# The White Envelope

# The White Envelope

Richard Vetere

**ABSOLUTELY AMAZING eBOOKS**

Published by Whiz Bang LLC, 926 Truman Avenue, Key West, Florida 33040, USA.



ISBN 978-1-951150-19-8

For information contact:
Publisher@AbsolutelyAmazingEbooks.com

“The truth is never pure and rarely simple.”

- Oscar Wilde

# The White Envelope

# 1

## 1963
## Ten Years Old

IT WAS JANUARY 1963 and right after my tenth birthday, that first Tuesday of the month my mother gave me a chore. Every Tuesday at four o'clock I was to walk up to Sixty-Fourth Street and pick up an envelope from my Aunt Josie who lived in a house in the middle of the block. I did it all that year, every week through every season.

Like the dutiful son I was, I'd walk up the steep hill called the Plateau in all kinds of weather cutting through the densely packed backyards while making my way past car garages and rows of hedges, bushes and small trees, all the while invisible to anyone around.

The walk only took about fifteen minutes with my short steps and awkward stride. I was just another kid out walking alone in the bleak autumn weather and most of the time there wasn't anyone around. Most men were working and their wives were either working also or picking their own kids up at school. The streets for the most part were deserted.

I was an unassuming looking short kid with a round face, short brown hair and big hazel eyes. When I look at photos from that time I'm never smiling. Instead I have no expression at all. If anything, I notice a look of bewilderment.

In most of the official school photos I'm wearing my Saint Stanislaus grammar school uniform of white shirt, blue slacks, tie and comfortable black shoes and other times a baseball uniform. Occasionally there's a photo with my mother and father where they look at me with pride and I continue to look perplexed at the camera.

I liked my chore it got me out in the fresh air after spending six hours in a classroom and then another hour or two in some kind of after school activity which mostly in the fall and winter months took place in the school auditorium.

Since fourth grade I walked home from school by myself making my way through the narrow European streets where the Polish lived and then up and over the new overpass and through Maurice Park and then down Maurice Avenue passed Mount Zion Cemetery that was so crowded they had stopped burying people there the year I was born.

As soon as I got home I'd headed out again and completed my errand, eventually making my way through the narrow alleyway that separated the two streets until I reached my Aunt Josie's house.

My Aunt Josie's house was wide and much larger than my parents'. It was pulled in from the sidewalk, rising up the west side of the Plateau with the rest of the street giving it a look of prestige unusual for the working class Queens neighborhood. It also had small gardens on both sides of the stoop and when it was summer large flowers bloomed and grass was everywhere there wasn't concrete.

Once on Sixty-Fourth Street I crossed, looking both ways even though there were no cars passing by, continuing my walk under the large elms standing tall along the sidewalk and then I walked up the two story cement stoop to the front door.

Every afternoon I'd stand face-to-face with the large front door to the two story brick house with its dark green awning over me and large overhanging concrete porch behind me and ring the bell.

My Aunt Josie would eventually open the door and after giving me a big smile and asking me how I was doing she'd hand me a white envelope. I would then turn around and walk the same way back home with the small white envelope clutched in my hand.

Once in my house I'd hand the envelope to my mother and she would place it on the dining room table for my father to take when he got home from work. Once he took it I never saw it again. If my mother wasn't home, I'd leave it on the table and by dinnertime it was gone.

My Aunt Josie wasn't actually my aunt. She was *not* a blood relation. However, many people had extended families and she was part of mine. She was a large, nearly obese, woman who had bad facial skin and died brown hair that never looked combed. She always had a cigarette dangling from her mouth. She had a pleasant voice and easy manner that made you like her.

I didn't know her well. My father and mother never spoke about her other than she was my aunt. I never asked questions because I was a child and I believed everything my parents told me. Everything around me made sense even when I was not sure it actually did.

Years later I heard my Aunt Josie was a local beauty queen for the Italian feast in Williamsburg. And years after that I was told that she only won the contest because someone owed her father a favor. None of it made any sense to me then or now. But it was what I had heard and I believed it all because I had no choice.

~ ~ ~

One Tuesday in November, after picking up the envelope for nearly a year, I reached her house like I had always done but this time after I rang her bell I noticed that the door was cracked open. I wasn't sure if I should enter the house but after a few moments I pushed the door back and walked into the living room.

Though the rooms in the house were large the house always seemed dark. The walls were painted some colorless off-white that never *seemed* white. The furniture was a dark wood, the rug a dark green and though there were windows the sunlight never seemed to make its way up high enough on the Plateau to share any daylight with the inside of the house.

Thinking back, I realize that I had only been in the rooms on the first floor a few times and I had never had a real look at anything inside.

But that afternoon, after pushing the door open, I walked into the living room and looked around. A large circular mirror was on one wall to my right, a dark green sofa below it, some chairs that looked deep, large and dark and a small brown table next to the sofa. I also saw my Aunt Josie on her back facing up at the ceiling with a large knife sticking out of the center of her chest.

I didn't move. I did take my time looking at her, wondering why she was on the floor with the knife in her chest. It was so dark in the room that if there was any blood, and I am sure there was, I didn't see any. What I did notice, was something I had never noticed about her before. She was wearing jewelry and a lot of it. I saw several rings on her immobile hands and a large silver necklace sprawled across her black blouse.

I'm not sure how long I stood there but I was about to turn and leave when I felt someone in the room with me beside my Aunt Josie. I was being watched. Someone in the shadow to my right was standing somewhere in the corner of the room in the dark, silently waiting for me to leave.

There is something about a house that makes you feel that it's occupied even when it's not. Or perhaps it's that all the lives lived in the house never truly leave and what you feel is the residue of lives lived. However, that day I felt someone real and very present scrutinizing me.

I didn't want to look directly where I thought they were so I stepped backwards to the door and then turned. I got to the first step on the way down and stopped. I had forgotten the envelope. I turned and took a long moment to study the front door which was still open. I wanted to leave but that obedient young boy, the one whose mother gave him a chore, felt compelled to complete it. So I walked back onto the concrete porch, faced the front door, and without taking a breath I stepped back into the house leaving the sun now low in the sky behind me.

I only got a foot or two into the living room before realizing I had no idea where to look for the envelope and more than that I was still sure I wasn't alone. My eyes scanned the shadows searching on the table near the sofa. Then I looked toward the kitchen through the designed hole in the wall that gave me a view of the kitchen. I wondered if the envelope could be on the kitchen table.

I was about to look when something made me glance down at my aunt and that's when I saw the envelope in her right hand. Her fingers were clinched around it. Whoever killed her probably got to her front door only minutes before I did. They probably rang the bell, or even walked in. She might have been in some other part of the house, saw the time on the large clock in the dining room that was around the corner of the wall, and figured it was *me* at the door.

I leaned down. I couldn't take my eyes off of the knife. It was small with a thick dark brown wooden handle. I reached over and grabbed the envelope and raced out of the house.

I ran all the way home feeling a fire at my back as if the flames were gaining on me. I didn't stop until I got to my own front door. I rang the bell. My mother answered. I handed her the envelope.

"What's wrong?" she asked.

"I think Aunt Josie's dead," I answered.

My mother called my father and my father called the police. But before they did all that they asked me exactly what I had seen when I went into the house. I told them every detail. They listened closely and then got quiet. My father told me that when a detective came to ask me what I had seen I shouldn't tell them about the envelope.

"Never talk about the envelope with anyone," my mother jumped in. "You never went to Aunt Josie's for anything ever before. You were there this afternoon only to pick up a chocolate cake she had baked for us. She liked to bake. Do you understand me, Mike?"

"But there was no cake there," I said.

"It doesn't matter," my mother answered.

My mother was pretty, but then all children probably think their parents are good looking, but she was. She had a heart shaped face, large deep brown eyes and soft brown hair that hugged the sides of her head, falling over her shoulders. She was petite but there was some inner strengthen that radiated from her quietness and her demeanor that even as I as a child I could sense.

Once, when I was very sick a few years earlier, I made the mistake of joining my cousins in a party at my house. That night I was shaking with fever and crying and my mother came to me in the middle of the night. She sat on the bed in the dark. I heard her steady voice without seeing her as she said, "I warned you. I hope you learned your lesson." And then she left.

I was more bewildered than ever but I nodded to her that night as I nodded to my parents that afternoon. She was my mother and together with my father they were my parents and I trusted them.

They watched me for a few moments, then shared a look between themselves and nodded to one another. My mother got me a glass of milk and a few cookies. She told me to go to my room so I did. I was an only child and I enjoyed the silence and peace of my own room. I had my own portable television set but I had homework to do so I did the one page math quiz on my desk.

It was nearly twilight when my mother called for me to come down the stairs. My father stood quietly beside her. He was a thin man with a receding hairline though he was probably not yet thirty-five. He had soft, light hazel eyes and delicate features but he was durable and kind.

"There is a detective outside who wants to talk to you. I told him that you would sit on the stoop and answer his questions," my mother said took my hand and led me to the door.

"Where will you be?" I asked.

"Right behind you," my father answered.

I opened the metal screen door since the main door was already opened.

I walked tentatively outside to a tall man who looked like he was wearing a sports jacket that was too tight and a tie that was too short.

He was also wearing a fedora. He smiled at me with his thin lips forced together. I said nothing but sat on the stoop and faced him. I liked sitting on the stoop. It gave me perspective and though I was sitting on brick I was comfortable there.

The man not only looked uncomfortable in his clothes he was uncomfortable in his own body.

"I'm Detective Walsh, Michael. Your mother and father told me what you told them about what you saw at your Aunt

Josie's house this afternoon. I have some officers up there now going through everything. Now can you tell me exactly what you saw?"

So I did. I told him everything. I told him how I went to pick up a chocolate cake from my aunt and how I found her dead on the floor.

I told the story watching Detective Walsh watching me. His eyes were small and light colored and they were focused on me so I decided to look right back at him.

Though I couldn't see them, I knew my parents were right on the other side of the door in the living room of our solid brick house. I knew they had a reason for me to lie so I lied.

"We didn't find any sign of cake in the house. Not in the kitchen. Nowhere."

I shrugged. "I took it when I left. I always liked the chocolate cake she baked." I wasn't lying about liking the cake.

He stepped closer. "You told your mother that your aunt was lying on her back. You told her that the door was already open when you got there. You told her that there was no one else in the house. Was there anything else you didn't tell her that you remember now?"

I looked closer at the detective. He hardly moved when he spoke. He stood there as if he was used to standing. He had both hands in his jacket pockets. I looked for his gun. I knew he had to have one. I imagined it was in a holster on his belt and I couldn't see because his jacket hid it.

"There was someone there. In the house."

He looked past me at my parents. He looked down at me. "What did they look like?"

"I don't know," I answered.

"What do you mean you don't know?"

"I didn't see them. But they were there."

He inched closer as if he wanted to not only look into my eyes but into my brain as well.

The light was fading and it was nearly dark. The light on top of the tall wooden lamp post popped on. It distracted me but it didn't affect him.

"How do you know anyone else was in that room if you didn't see them?"

I looked up at him allowing him to look directly into my eyes and my brain if he wanted to. "I felt it. Like a ghost. You can't see them but they're there."

An odd expression crossed his face. Half smile, half smirk. He rubbed his forehead with his hand and looked over me at the front door.

"Thank you, Mrs. Tucci," he said to where my mother had been standing out of sight on the other side of the screen. He looked at me. "You're brave. I hope you don't have any nightmares tonight. Goodbye, Michael."

I watched him strut down the small walkway between the two rows of hedges my father had planted that led to the sidewalk. I watched him walk to a parked car and then I turned around, waiting for him to drive away.

Once I got inside, my father hugged me and my mother sat me down on the sofa and patted my head. "You are brave," she said softly.

Shadows filled the room. My father turned on a lamp; nobody said a word. Nobody moved, not even me.

That was the extent of my memory of that afternoon and the interrogation that followed. I do remember asking my parents about the chocolate cake and why I had to lie, but they told me that it was okay and that there was nothing to worry about. It was all over now.

They were right since a few days later the first and only Catholic president of the United States was shot and killed in Dallas. The nuns told all the students while we were in school and they cried hysterically as they did. They decided to let us go home early. Once we saw the nuns crying we cried along with them, glad to be let home early to retreat to the safety of our families.

When he got home from work I asked my father why they killed the president and my father told me that it was because he was Catholic.

The entire world seemed focused on the assassination and my Aunt Josie's murder was forgotten. It was never mentioned again in my house and the police went on to something else.

Never again did I have to walk up to her house to pick up a white envelope and her murder remained an unsolved crime for fifty years.

# 2

## 1973
## Twenty Years Old

I'M TELLING THIS STORY now because it has occurred to me after all these decades that what happened that afternoon, and the reasons that it did, had an invisible yet profound effect on my life.

I am pretty sure most of us really don't know much about ourselves other than the obvious and even those qualities and essences are usually as vague as our memories after time.

We rely on those closest to us to tell us about ourselves. We rely on family and lovers to give us insight into who we are.

Perhaps that is why we need God. We need some entity to forgive us, look out for us and give us guidance even if only through the lens of faith.

However, what happens if we can't trust family or lovers to tell us the truth? What happens if they aren't there anymore or perhaps they are unable to for whatever reasons? Then we only have our own perceptions and our own memories to disable secrets and make sense out of codes and mysteries.

I purposefully didn't go back to that house for a decade. It was a party in the summer of 1972 that brought me back. Since my Aunt Josie didn't have any children her older cousin Louis bought the house from the estate lawyers. My aunt did have a husband, Frank, but he died in jail was all of what I knew.

My aunt's cousin Louis ran a construction business and bought my Aunt Josie's business from her estate and blended it into his own. Though I hardly knew his son, Louis, Jr., I did meet him a few times over the years at family events when my parents brought me along. So, I was surprised to get an invitation to his engagement party which I went to one warm summer night. The party was being thrown in his backyard. My parents were away on a vacation in Florida, so they couldn't go.

I was twenty years old and I had changed significantly from when I was a kid. I have no idea how or why but I was no longer the compliant, chubby child I had been. Some hormone kicked in and my demeanor changed. I was now rebellious and confident. Physically I was no longer the round faced cherub. I was lanky and sexual with waves of curly brown hair falling over my shoulders. My face was angular though I was still slight with small shoulders and a tiny waist. People told me that I had a hungry look in my eyes; and I was hungry. I was hungry for knowledge, hungry for experience and starving for recognition, though for what I wasn't exactly sure.

My round eyes which once looked out at the world with bewilderment now looked at the world with a sharply focused curiosity. I was also going to the local college and was recently made literary editor of the student magazine. I had published a poem in a national magazine, *Perspectives*, and suddenly I was a literary star on campus. My poetry was philosophical in nature, romantic in scope, introspective and as refined as any young talent could be at that time; fighting popular culture by doing all they could to ignore it. However, the paradox was that the more I fought it, the more I yearned for it.

So, I was young and directionless with only the love of poetry to drive me through the long arduous days of college life.

Louis Jr. called and invited me to his birthday party. Though I knew his friends would all be wearing suits with open shirts and gold chains dangling from their necks and soft patent leather shoes and silk socks, I'd wear my jeans with the bell-bottoms and my dungaree jacket and my dark blue T-shirt, cowboy boots and no socks.

I also wore colored wrist bands and a one percent purple patch on the right sleeve of my jacket. It stood for the one percent of motorcycle riders who were outlaws. Though I did ride a blue Triumph I certainly wasn't a *percenter* but it felt good to pretend to be one. It felt good to lie.

So, I was all prepared for the party that Friday night and looking forward to it but the only thing I wasn't prepared for was meeting *her*.

The moment I saw her she made me feel comfortable even though I had never seen her before. She wasn't a college student, she was a woman. She was wearing a silk blue dress that stuck to her as if it never wanted to let go of her womanly shape. When she moved her entire being moved with her. I had never met anyone so *female* before. She was feminine in every way.

She had thick black hair that fell to both sides of her face, hugging her cheeks, and her large violet eyes radiated seduction. Every male in the backyard was looking at her along with some women as well.

The moment I saw her I was jealous of anyone who knew her name. I wanted to know everything about her, where she was born, what she liked and disliked, and most importantly why I had never met her before.

I had to walk over to her and I did. She was standing with Louis Jr. and when he introduced her to me she smiled and kept looking. She didn't turn away. It was reassuring. Women liked looking at me. Like I said, I was no longer the cherub.

"This is Christine, my fiancée," Louis Jr. said.

"Michael," I said to her.

All had gone black for a moment. I couldn't believe she was engaged to him.

After I said hello and she smiled at me, she turned back to Louis Jr. It was then that I noticed they were holding hands. I now knew why he had the party. He wanted to show off his prize. On the other hand, I had no idea why he had invited me.

Louis Jr. was a large young man. He had a small head with delicate features with small diamond colored blue eyes. It was clear that he pampered himself from the cologne he wore to the silk suits and linen white shirts.

Louis Jr. pulled Christine away and I found myself alone.

All through the night I kept looking Christine's way wanting to get closer, wanting to talk to her. Late in the night I noticed Louis Jr. walk out of the backyard by his father's side for what I figured was business talk and I maneuvered myself to be at her side.

Of course, by then, I was unable to even attempt a conversation. So, she walked away and I was again alone.

For the first time I allowed myself to look around. Blue, yellow, red and green lights had been strung everywhere like Christmas decorations hanging from the small recently built metal gazebo and they hung along the metal fence that lined both sides of the yard.

Since the house was on the Plateau there was a hill at furthest end of the backyard and beyond that a wall. Beyond the wall was a large empty lot inhabited by small trees and stones and beyond that the backyards of the row of houses on top of the Plateau.

It was then, standing alone and looking up at the lit windows of the homes above, that it all hit me. I had found my aunt murdered in this house. Of course, I knew that it happened but it was something I didn't dwell on or think about over the years. When I drove past the house it was infrequently and most of the time I didn't exhaust myself with thoughts about the events that took place that afternoon.

Now, with the colored lights beaming from the fence and hedges surrounding the yard, the blasting music, the dancing, the conversations and all the pretty people having fun in the party atmosphere, it felt so odd to even try and imagine what happened on that bleak November afternoon.

I walked past the happy faces; the well-dressed young men and women in the party dresses, and left the bright lights of the backyard and walked along the side of the house. The light in the walkway between her house and the other to my right was subdued.

There was a small lamp above the door that led to the kitchen and that's all there was. I walked through the shadows which hugged the side of the house and headed to the very edge of the brick wall, turning left to the front door.

I was under the canopy and in seconds I was facing the same closed door and again it was open. This time music played in the night air and though the night felt festive, I didn't. Yet that wasn't going to stop me. I walked into the house and entered the living room.

I looked down. For a moment I thought I saw my aunt lying there with the knife in her chest. For a moment I felt as if someone was watching me just like I felt that afternoon.

A hand poked my shoulder. I shuddered.

"Sorry!" I heard a woman say.

I turned. It was Christine standing behind me. I could see from the look on her face that she knew.

"Louis just told me," she said.

I looked down. My aunt was gone as if she had never been there. *Ever*.

"I had heard the story so many times. I always thought how awful. And I wondered about the boy. That poor boy. And it is *you*," she said. Her sympathy was sincere.

I made a face of some kind and turned and walked out onto the concrete porch. The wide porch was actually the roof of the garage below.

I looked up at the black sky and the splattering of stars. Down below the cement flower pots that lined the edge of the porch was the street lit by lampposts.

Christine stood beside me. "I'm sorry if I embarrassed you."

"You didn't," I said. "I was kind of locked in something I was remembering just now. That's why I jumped."

"You want a drink?" she asked.

"I'm okay," I answered. "It was a long time ago," I told her. "I hadn't been up here for years. I actually forgot about it, I think. Or maybe I didn't want to think about it. It's almost like it happened to someone else and not me."

"When I first heard the story, I figured the person I was hearing about must have moved far away from here," she said.

I shrugged my shoulders. "Where would I go? This is my home," I told her gesturing to the world below the porch.

"There you are," Louis Jr. said. Seconds later he was standing with us. "I didn't think you'd come," he said to me. "You know, being here and all that."

"He doesn't think about it," Christine told him and then looked at me.

"He's got to think about it. He found her," Louis said. Now he was looking at me.

"Hey, man, let's talk about something else. It's your party," I told them forcing a smile, and in minutes we were in the backyard and I was pushing back a memory that I thought I had already forgotten.

Before I could move Louis Jr. stopped me. "Oh, my father wants to talk to you."

Moments later I was facing Louis Sr. He was a bulky man with thinning grey hair and small diamond blue eyes just like his son. He was wearing a black silk shirt with white stripes which stuck to his big belly making it seem as if it were painted on. "Michael, it was my idea to invite you," he said to me. "I knew my cousin would want you here."

I nodded and thanked him for thinking of me. He asked me a lot of questions about my life, complimenting me on how good I looked and then told me he wanted me to meet someone who had been asking about me. That was when I met Ted.

Earlier in the night when I was taking to a friend of Louis Jr.'s I noticed someone watching me from the makeshift bar. He was tall and thin with pepper gray hair neatly cut and combed. He was older than me and probably more my parent's age.

He wore a powder blue jacket and light blue shirt and like all the other men there he had the exterior of someone gregarious, looking for fun and probably drinking too much scotch.

After Louis Sr. introduced us he said, "I know your parents. From your Aunt Josie."

It was the first time anyone mentioned her name to me. I took a closer look at him. Though he had handsome features he had this expression that made him look irritated even when he smiled. His eyes were oval and dark brown, giving the illusion of two circular pools.

During the night I caught him looming in my direction as if studying me. When Louis Sr. eventually introduced us Ted spoke to me with an odd sense of glee. I couldn't explain it in any other way. His oval eyes were strangely inviting.

As we stood in a circle Ted narrowed his shoulders, edging closer to me until he was directly in front of me blocking out the best he could any view I had of anyone including Christine, who was the one person at the party that I did want to speak with.

"It must have been difficult finding her that way," Ted said.

I didn't respond and he didn't really seem to want an answer from me.

"You were so young to see death up close like that."

I nodded. I was perplexed wondering why I had the sudden sense that I knew this man. I couldn't place where I knew him but he felt alarmingly familiar as if he was a peril from my past that I had completely forgotten; perhaps like how I had blocked out seeing my aunt lying motionless on her living room floor.

"You said you know my parents," I said.

"I do. From years ago. Through the family. I know Louis Sr. from our days back in Brooklyn."

I knew that Ted meant Williamsburg since that was where my mother was from. She was born and grew up on Lorimar Street right across from McCarran Park.

"You grew up to be a good-looking kid," he said to me.

"You knew me then?"

"Of course I did. You don't remember, do you?" he asked.

I shook my head.

"I picked you up one day at the bus stop when you were on your way to school and the bus was late. I drove you to school," he said.

I fought hard to remember when suddenly a scene flashed in my mind. I remember a man in a car reaching his head out the passenger side window in the rain talking to me. But that was all that came to my mind.

"We had a nice talk," he said. The slight inflection in his voice made what he said sound like a lie.

I shook my head and now I lied. "I don't remember."

He nodded and gave me a small smile. "That's okay. Look, I invited Louis Jr. and Christine to my place next weekend. I'll make sure they bring you," he said. "I'm having a party just to have a party."

He then quickly moved back to the same place he had been standing before he had edged closer to me. I found myself face to face with Christine. "So he told you about his party?"

"Yes."

"You'll come?" she smiled.

"If you go, I'll go," I smiled back.

She pursued her lips and relaxed her smile. "Don't you have a girl?"

"No one special," I told her.

Not long after the party ended, and I went home to my small apartment in Bayside and had a restless sleep about a man in a car, a face peering through the rain and then, as if watching it all from a short distance away, I saw a small boy holding a lunch box get into a car at a bus stop. The car then drove away.

When I woke up I realized I was the little boy who got into the car. I got out of bed and put on the lights and then the TV. I couldn't sleep the rest of the night.

# 3

## 1960
## Seven Years Old

I WAS STANDING ON THE BUS STOP in the rain waiting for the bus to take me to school. I was eight years old and nothing more than a wingless angel. The world was a dark, gray place and I was a cog in the wheel of my known cosmos, struggling through it without freedom and without choice. I did recall being told when to go to sleep, when to wake up, what to do with my time and what I should think. I know I must have experienced some joy but I don't remember it.

Ironically, even if I was the master of my own universe I wouldn't know what to do with the power. I saw the people around me as fierce but incapacitated human beings overwhelmed with duties and responsibilities.

So I gave in. I allowed my delicate amebic soul to be the obedient servant to the authorities who dictated every nuance of my behavior. If I had a notion of what the future would be like I have no memory of dwelling on it. I could only see as far as the following day and perhaps to the end of the week but that was it.

I'm sure I was genderless, though women fascinated me. Females my age who I came across in school even then seemed to me so much more in control of their lives than I was. They strutted through the hallways and the schoolyard talking and sharing laughs with other girls. They put a lot more attention into their clothing and their looks than I ever thought about.

On the other hand, the boys my age came across to me as brutes. They were loud, obnoxious and physical in so many ways I could never be. They didn't seem to think or reflect on anything. I wasn't sure if they were in denial or just stupid.

Besides the girls in class, older women fascinated me even more so. At my age then they were probably those in their late teens who entered my life at various times for various reasons.

~ ~ ~

Sometimes there would be a babysitter and other times the sister or friend of a babysitter. Nothing sexual ever happened but they were there in my peripheral vision, lingering joyously on the outskirts of my life. I noticed how they smiled and laughed boldly with confidence, even more so than the girls in school. All the while I yearned for the same recklessness.

One of the things I do remember of that time was about my mother. I remember the sponge baths she gave me in the kitchen sink before we had a tub in our bathroom. It was one place we seemed to connect and in many ways it was probably because it was one of those times in my life that for short moments it was all about me.

I would be filled with glee as I'd bounce around in the sink looking up at mother wondering why she was so serious. She'd speak to me but nothing she said ever registered. I was king in that sink, enraptured by the warm liquid, bubbly universe engulfing me.

A few years later I asked my mother if I could help her dye her hair. With my babysitter Maureen I'd watch as she would first wash my mother's long brown hair in the sink and then have my mother sit in a chair and drape several towels over her.

Maureen would then apply the hair darkener and that was when I was allowed to help. With my mother leaning forward in the chair I'd smooth the lush brown shampoo into my mother's thick hair.

It was entirely sensual for me. Having her long, dark hair in my fingers pushing, the copious brown dye deep into her roots. My mother's silence and Maureen's voice softly giving me directions helped me lose myself in the chore.

That was our Friday night ritual and during it I can honestly say I felt entirely androgynous. I felt perhaps like a child-woman without desire.

I was plump, undesirable and asexual. With my big eyes, short haircut and chubby cheeks I was the cherub and not much else. That was the Michael of those years and the most sensual experience of that time was soaking my mother's hair as I helped her darken it to make her beautiful.

~ ~ ~

I wasn't sure how long I was waiting when a car pulled up to the bus stop and the curb. I remember a man leaning forward through the passenger side window and talking to me. He said something about the bus being delayed and that he could drive me to school. He told me he knew my parents and he called me *Michael.*

So, I got into the car. I didn't even hesitate. I was a good kid who didn't want to be late and I trusted all the adults in my life. I had no reason not to.

When I got into the car he drove off and was smoking a cigarette. He drove in the direction of the school but veered off and drove directly to Grand Avenue but further north of the school. He then parked.

I looked around and saw that we were in a parking lot. I looked up at him. Neither of us said a word the entire drive. He looked at me with an oddly troubled expression.

I remember the rain falling hard on the windshield, splashing and flying in every direction, and I still remember holding my umbrella waiting for him to say or do anything which would then give me an idea on what to say back to him. Yet he just looked at me.

I knew where I was. My school was a long walk down Grand Avenue. I thought perhaps he was driving me as far as he could and it was up to me to get there on my own. I opened the door.

"Close that," he said sharply.

I did.

"Where do you think you're going?" he asked.

"School," I answered.

He looked straight ahead into the rain. "Do you know who I am?"

"You said you know my parents."

He nodded. "I do." I then remember him reaching for me. After that, I have no further memory of that morning at all.

# 4

## 1960
## Seven Years Old

IT WAS A SUNDAY AFTERNOON in June. My father was napping on the sofa and I was playing with him. Though he was trying to nap I was throwing pillows at him. Despite his being exhausted from a long week of work as a clerk in Manhattan he was being very congenial with me and did not lose his temper even though he asked me nicely to stop.

Hearing what was going on my mother appeared from the kitchen and took me aside. She had already asked me several times to stop and I had ignored her.

So, this time she fixed her gaze on me and said, “Don’t you ever think I will ever chose you over your father, do you understand me?”

I was shocked. I didn’t know how to react. I searched her warm, brown eyes for a hint that perhaps she was joking with me but all I got back was a white heat of indignation as if to dare me to find any humor in her statement.

Up to that moment in my life I believed I was the king of my domain. I was much loved by all and within our house and its borders I came first and I was the center of its universe. Until that moment, that is.

I didn’t respond but retreated to my room and hid until an hour later my mother came to me to announce that we were going out.

She dressed me in a powder blue shirt with white vertical strips and beige shorts. She made me wear knee high socks and white sneakers. With my short hair and the sheepish look on my face I felt ridiculous. I was a slave to her fashion whims.

Not long after we were walking through the translucent afternoon light up the Plateau to my Aunt Josie's house. I learned it was Louis Jr.'s confirmation and we had to make an appearance. "I wish your father could come with us. He wants to rest," my mother told me. She was wearing a light dress with white heels. I can remember her carrying a gift. It was a box nearly wrapped in gold paper with red ribbon.

She held my hand as we walked along the tree lined sidewalk. "I wish I had a better dress to wear. They are so rich up there. They'll probably talk about what I'm wearing."

I was startled by her sharing with me her thoughts. I believed my mother looked like a princess. I had no idea she had such insecurities.

I couldn't think of anyone lovelier or more graceful. I averted my eyes making sure we didn't make eye contact. I was embarrassed by her revelation. I had no idea she thought other people had more than us.

I'm pretty sure she didn't want a response. She just looked ahead and walked toward the house. I felt her pride more than anything else and yet when we walked up those concrete steps to the front door she gripped my hand and she gripped it even tighter as we entered the backyard.

Like Louis Jr.'s engagement party many years later there were colored lights strung along the solid brick house and there was music playing. Though I didn't know then I am sure now it was Sinatra and probably Dean Martin playing on a Victrola sitting on a table with wires running into the house to give it the electricity.

I stayed close to my mother's side as we moved through the backyard among all the party goers. I listened closely to conversations trying to decipher if anyone mentioned anything about my mother's dress.

At one point I was forced to say hello to Louis Jr. who was a chubby kid back then with slicked back hair and a loud mouth. He hardly acknowledged me and seemed to prefer instead to throw rocks at a black cat that was racing along the fence in the short grass.

Beside him were his cousins Joey Parisi and Charlie Durrico, just as jovial and just as obnoxious as they laughed loudly when they managed to hit the cat. They laughed even more heartily when it jumped.

My Aunt Josie saw what was going on and yelled at them and for some reason turned to me. I could see a tenderness in her eyes radiating at me like a warm light. "He's not like them," she said to my mother.

My mother kissed Aunt Josie on the cheek and I could hear my mother say softly, "He's doing fine in school."

My aunt smiled at her. "Connie, you're doing a great job bringing him up. You should be proud of yourself. Michael is a good boy."

Just at that moment I saw Ted for the first time. Of course, I didn't know who he was then and nor would I be able to know that a couple of years later he'd be the man picking me up in the car on the bus stop that rainy morning.

Ted was looking down on me and smiling. He might have been handsomer then but I'm not sure. He had the same glint in his eye when he looked at me though he had this wall around him. I felt that same isolation when I saw him over a decade later at Louis Jr.'s engagement party in this same backyard.

A young woman stepped up to my Aunt Josie and spoke to her and my mother. She was very pretty and exuded a brand new sexual energy that I didn't know existed.

She had curly thick black hair and wore a black leather jacket and jeans and she had a friend at her side that was just as sexy with long red hair in a blue jacket and in jeans.

I had been standing next to my mother but then found a chair so I sat down facing the four women observing and hoping to learn something. They captivated me like glittering gold pieces in the sand. I had to control my scrutiny hoping not to be hypnotized by their very appearance.

The one with the thick curly hair said that she had lost her car keys. The four women were eager to help her find them.

I had noticed that while she was talking she unconsciously placed them in her small handbag.

"They're in your bag," I said, my tiny voice hardly breaking through the din of the party.

But my mother heard me. "Michael said to check your bag."

The young woman with the curly hair gave me a glance then opened up her handbag and pulled out her keys.

All four women looked with wonder at the cherub in the chair with his pulled-up socks and shorts looking like a baby King Tut surveying the females in his domain.

Thrilled that her keys weren't lost she stepped over to me. "Thank you, little man," she said.

Mother was perplexed, her lips twisted. My Aunt Josie patted me on the head. "How wonderful, isn't he?" she announced.

The only other memory I have of that afternoon was the look on my mother's face when she saw Ted. He was standing way in the corner of the backyard against the iron grated fence talking to some of my aunt's relatives.

I felt her grip my hand when they exchanged looks. It was a different grip though from when we first walked into the backyard. That time she was holding on to me for comfort and support *this* time she held my hand as if not wanting to let go of me; as if I would be ripped from her by some force of nature.

I didn't know how to respond. I was a child and the moment was out of the realm of my comprehension.

We left the party immediately after that leaving whatever transpired silently between Ted and my mother behind us.

All along our walk back in the fading sunlight my mother looked over her shoulder keeping me one step ahead of her never once letting go of my hand.

When home she put me in my room. I heard her and my father in the living room downstairs taking in hushed voices. I slipped out of my room and sat on the stairs hidden by shadows the sunset was creating and listened intently.

"You have to talk to her," my mother said.

They were out of sight but our house was so quiet I could hear every word and as long as I placed my small body behind our large banister I couldn't be seen.

"I don't want him around our son."

There was a long silence. My father was probably sitting up on the sofa and my mother was probably sitting in her favorite chair to the right of the sofa.

"It's not like her to not think ahead. I don't know why she invited him," my father said.

"She doesn't think that woman. Sometimes she doesn't think. The whole family is like that. They're loud and they like to show off their money."

Again silence. My father spoke in the soft voice he always spoke to her with when she was angry or frustrated. "Connie, it will be okay. It was only this one time."

"That's not what I want to hear, Ed, it's not what I want to hear."

"Did Mike notice?" father asked.

"He's a child. The only thing he had his eyes on were the teenagers."

"Girls, I hope."

"Yes, what do you think? Of course, he has his eyes on the girls."

It got very quiet. Usually at times like that when I happened to walk in on them I'd find them kissing. So, I took the advantage of the moment and slipped back up the stairs to my room leaving my parents to do what it was they liked to do when I wasn't around.

Back in my room I forgot all about Ted but I did think a lot about the young woman with the curly dark hair and how exciting it was to reveal that she had her keys in her handbag and how thrilling it was to get her full attention.

That was my life up to that time. It was still a couple of years before I'd be taking those trips to my aunt's house to pick up the white envelope.

# 5

## 1973
## Twenty Years Old

WHEN I SAW MY MOTHER and father at dinner one night a few days later I told them I met someone named Ted who said he knew them.

Their reaction was strange. My mother looked at me without blinking and my father's small hazel eyes widened. "How is he?" my father asked.

I persisted in asking how they knew him and they told me that he was my Aunt Josie's friend from the old neighborhood and then they changed the conversation. I let it drop and went on with my life never expecting to hear from him again.

That was the way it was until I got a call from Louis Jr. inviting me to a party at Ted's penthouse apartment in Manhattan the following Friday night. I agreed to go.

As soon as I got to his address I knew Ted had to have money. He lived on Central Park South, which back in the '70s seemed like a barren and even impersonal row of hotels and apartment buildings.

However, once the doorman let me in and I was told to go to the penthouse on the twentieth floor.

The elevator opened. There was only one apartment on the entire floor. I walked to the door and found it open.

Once inside I faced a sunken living room and the dim lights and music from a stereo. The sunken living room had large bay windows revealing a view of Central Park.

There were rock posters of The Who, Cream and some obscure but terrific British blues bands like Savoy Brown hanging in frames on the surrounding walls.

The song *Brandy* by the Looking Glass was playing as I walked deeper into the apartment.

The first person I saw was Christine. Dressed in jeans and black halter top appropriate for the summer, she greeted me with a warm hug.

"You made it."

I smiled back.

Behind Christine, Central Park stretched into the darkness. We were twenty stories above street level and though I didn't spend much time in Manhattan I enjoyed my time there even though the city was wallowing in its own decay and close to financial bankruptcy.

Nothing was what it used to be. The city was like a loose fitting dream of steel and only the wealthy thrived in it; and the very poor.

I kissed Christine on the cheek and saw Louis Jr. lingering behind her, eyeing our greeting. He was on us in seconds but not before Christine's hand purposely caressed mine for a moment. I made eye contact. She didn't blink and allowed my glance to linger before she turned to Louis Jr. to give him her full attention.

When I was a teenager I had my favorite crawl space. It was in our small concrete backyard. At the very corner that faced a truck lot there was a tool shack with a narrow area between the wooden shack and a large fence.

I used to sit in the narrow space and think about my future. I conjured a dark haired woman who would come into my life and save me. It was the gender reverse of Prince

Charming. She would be a princess or an heiress and I'd be this sensitive poet and she would pull me out of the depths of my working class world.

Looking at Christine at that very moment I wondered if she was the dark-haired beauty I had imagined.

Ted distracted me when he appeared stepping out from his bedroom wearing a white cloth shirt that made him look like a high priest of Cossack origins.

He had a large joint and handed it to Christine. Beyond him I saw three other couples but no one I recognized. They were all sitting in a circle smoking hashish which I could smell the minute I walked into the apartment.

Soon I was sitting in the circle with Christine on one side of me and Ted on the other. The lights were dim and outside you could see the glimmering lights from uptown making it look as if they were stars.

*Nights in White Sati*n by the Moody Blues was playing on the stereo and I was stoned. I still remember Christine being so close to me I had to continue to look away. A couple in front of me was kissing and another was doing more than that.

A blond waif in jeans and a peasant shirt, barefoot, allowed the thin young man she was with to lay on top of her. I could see her pulling his jeans back over his bottom and Ted said to me, "Love the one you're with."

I looked at him and realized that he and I completed the symmetrical balance of couples. There were ten of us.

The next thing I remember was Ted leaning in and handing me some acid. I downed it with a glass of wine.

"I got a surprise for us," he said leaning in. He stood up. "Come with me."

I turned to Christine and took her hand. I was more than surprised when she held it and followed me. However, my surprise went away when I saw that Louis Jr. was sitting beside the waif-like blond licking her voluptuous bare breast.

Christine didn't react instead she nodded to me to follow Ted.

Ted opened the door and Christine and I followed him into a semi-darkened room. Sitting with their legs folded behind large pillows were two young women.

Stoned on the acid I found myself in a circle again but this time we were all kissing and fondling. I was thrilled to find Christine's lips and I took in her breath and felt her hand grip my shoulder.

I don't know how long we kissed and I can't remember what happened to everyone else but I do remember Louis Jr. storming into the room grabbing my shoulder and pushing me away.

I was lying on my side realizing I was shirtless and Louis Jr. was in his boxer shorts and his round fleshy belly bouncing in the soft light.

Christine was fully dressed and Ted was on his back howling with glee as Louis Jr. stood over Christine his mouth open wide. "You slut!"

"You call me that?" Christine shot back at him. "What were you doing with that blond?" She pushed him away. "Leave me alone."

Louis Jr. was the type of man who had no shame. Today they'd call him a narcissist or perhaps an egomaniac who believed he was always right. The world's opinion meant nothing to him.

I suppose the acid had taken control of me since all I could concentrate on was the pool of watery light coming from the other side of the window. I wasn't sure if it were raining or that I had sunk down to the bottom of the sea but I was sure of one thing and that was Christine had kissed me.

Oddly when she kissed me I saw my aunt lying on her living room floor with the knife in her chest.

I shook my head. I felt someone standing in the shadows in the living room. I wanted to peek around the darkness and see who it was.

"Is it me?" I asked.

"Is *who* you?" I heard Christine ask.

"Standing in the shadows. Is that me? Am I watching myself? Am I there? Did I see who killed her? I need to know," I told her surprising even myself.

I turned to Christine. I could see a look of horror on her face. She held me.

The acid killed any more specific recollection of that night other than Christine and I found a place to sleep side by side but we were too stoned to do anything more than drift in and out of consciousness.

When we did wake up we found Ted was in a dead sleep in his bedroom. Both Christine and I hardly said anything to one another that morning.

We walked outside both looking worn out from the acid and lack of sleep. There were dark circles under her eyes and her hair was stringy. I kissed her on the cheek and put her in a cab not knowing that I wouldn't see her for a while.

But right before I did I touched her face. "You look like my mother," I told her.

~ ~ ~

I didn't hear from her again for over a year and when I did it was Ted who called me telling me she was getting married to Louis Jr.

"Do you want to go to the wedding?" he asked.

"I don't want to go," I lied. I knew how to lie but this time it hurt because I wanted nothing more than to see her even if she was in a wedding gown.

"If you change your mind, let me know. You can come as my guest," he said.

I hung up and paced my small apartment. I felt as if I had been abandoned by someone I was hoping to get to know more deeply than anyone I had ever known.

~ ~ ~

I went to the wedding but not the party. I drove my motorcycle to the church and parked across the street waiting for the bride to come walking out of the church doors.

Christine looked beautiful in her flowing white dress and Louis Jr. looked like some useless appendage to the entire event.

I prayed for rain and fog and even lightening but all I got was a gorgeous cool morning with abundant sunshine like the weatherman always says.

I was hoping Christine would see me but she was barraged by rice and cheers. I got on my motorcycle and faced the overwhelming loneliness of the rest of the day alone.

# 6

## 1998
## Forty-Five Years Old

DETECTIVE MANNY LAMBISI was my age but he looked a decade older. I had put on a few pounds since I was in my early forties. In fact, I had put on more than a few pounds. I added over twenty. My hairline was receding and I wore glasses. However, the extra fat brought back the cherub in me since the extra weight gave me a baby face.

I did have broad shoulders from years of weight training but I did very little physical activity since I had become a writer. I wrote historical fiction and I continued to write and publish poetry. I taught in some excellent English departments in the Tri-State area.

Despite my physical failings I was pleased with how my life had turned out so far.

The day Manny called me from the 112th Precinct he told me he was part of the Cold Case Squad and he wanted to talk to me about my Aunt Josie's murder.

I agreed to drive to the precinct and the desk sergeant told me to go up the stairs to the detective squad on the second floor.

To enter the squad first you had to go through a locked door and you had to be buzzed in. Once inside that door you had to push aside a smaller waist high door.

The décor in the room was antiquated. The office had the kind of furniture you saw in movies from the 1940s. The only thing that was contemporary was a color television in one corner and computers on all the desks.

I asked the first detective I came across for Detective Lambisi. He pointed me in the direction of a hunched over man in a dark sports jacket suit and tie sitting at a desk so I walked over to him.

Manny had that tired look some middle-aged people have that makes you wonder what they had been doing with their lives. You wondered if they ever slept at all and if they did, did they ever get any rest.

He had thick black magic marker circles under his eyes and though he too had broad shoulders like me his shoulders looked much like a span to a bridge in need of serious repair. They looked like they were about to collapse at any moment by the weight of not was there particularly at the time but what had crossed over them years earlier.

Once I sat and he thanked me for taking the time to see him he opened up an old file and placed it on his desk in front of me.

Facing him I also noticed that Manny had a very deep red blotch of skin under his chin.

He noticed me looking.

"It's a skin rash. Eczema. I had it since I was a kid. Seems there are some things you never get rid of no matter how old you get," he stated drolly as if making a point about me though talking about himself.

"What happened to the detective who interviewed me?" I asked changing the subject.

"Detective Walsh died in 1988. This is his file," Manny stated. He had an odd voice. It wasn't a baritone and it wasn't a soprano. In fact, it was bland. The only distinction it had for me was that the tone was purely cynical.

He looked me straight in the eyes. He had murky brown ones with dark eyebrows. "We opened up the file. I know it's been a while but sometimes it takes decades to find a killer. What is working for us is that Mayor Giuliani merged the transit and housing cops. We're up to forty-five thousand NYPD now. That means more of us are working the cold cases. That's how I got this case," he explained.

"Okay," I said.

He gestured to Walsh's notebook. "So according to Detective Walsh's notes it was you who found her."

"Yes, I found her."

"Lying on her back in the living room right at the door. She had a knife in her chest."

"Yes to everything you just said."

"What were you doing up there that day?" he asked now changing his tone from neutral to something else.

I almost smiled but stopped myself. "Picking up a chocolate cake."

He sat back and *he* smiled but it wasn't the reflection of a happy feeling. It was more like a grimace with sarcastic intentions. "Nobody believes that."

"Nobody believes *what* exactly?" I asked.

"Nobody believes that you were up there to pick up a cake."

"Who's nobody?" I asked matching his cynical tone with a sarcastic one of my own.

"Why were you *really* there, Mister Tucci?" he asked directly.

"My aunt was a great cook," I answered. "And she baked a great chocolate cake."

He looked away. "She wasn't actually a blood relative but you called her Aunt Josie, why is that?"

"She and my mother were close friends. And to answer your question I don't know why we did that kind of thing back then. But that's what Italian families did back then. Everybody close was a relative."

"How come you never moved?" he asked me.

I shrugged. "What does that have to do with anything?" I asked him.

"You live in your parent's house is that correct?"

"Yes, they left it to me? Why?"

"You know that saying about returning to the scene of the crime," he said not as a question but as a fact.

"What does that have to do with me?" I asked him.

He ignored my question by asking me another of his own. "How tall were you then?"

I shrugged. "I have no idea."

He placed an old slip of paper he took from the file and placed it in front of me. "This is something Detective Walsh put in the file. I am figuring you were measured back at your grammar school for something. Read it for me please," he said.

The piece of paper was yellow and about two inches wide and three inches long. I still had good eyesight and read it closely. "Michael Tucci. Five feet one and three quarter inches."

"Turn it over," he told me.

I saw a signature. "Sister Mary Anchletus," I said aloud. I then read the date underneath the signature. "The twenty-eight of January nineteen sixty-one."

I was puzzled. "Where did he get this?" I asked.

"Down at the parish probably."

"So you know how tall I was? What does that mean?"

"Your *Aunt* Josie was five foot even." He nodded, scratching his chin and sitting back.

"And that means *what*?"

"You were tall enough to stab her."

Now I smirked. But I kept silent. I was getting it now. They had no suspects and figured why not make me one?

"That's crazy. I was a kid."

"We got our share of kid murderers in this city."

I studied him again. He stopped looking at me directly. He was grabbing for straws. "Okay, go with your thought. Why would I want to kill my aunt?"

"You tell me," he said, now *looking* directly at me.

I kept silent.

"Look, I am asking about the cake for one reason, okay?"

"Okay."

"I know you lied about the chocolate cake. And no one lies about something that obvious unless they are hiding something else and usually that is the important *thing* they are lying about."

"And my parents were in on it too?" I said humoring him.

"Yeah, they'd have to be," he answered.

I didn't respond.

Manny sat back and looked out the window to his left but he had to strain his neck to do so since his desk wasn't exactly lined up to a window. It was sunny out and I could see that he craved sunlight probably from a lack of getting much of it.

"I have been reading Walsh's report and over and over again I see this nonsense about chocolate cake and I keep asking myself why you told him that. Tell me. Why were you *really* at her house?"

"I told you *why* I was there."

"Walsh has eye witnesses, your aunt's neighbors who told him that they saw you at her door every Tuesday after school," Manny said. "Did you go to her house for this cake *every* Tuesday?"

I moved in my chair. It all felt surreal. After all these years no one had asked me anything about my aunt's death since that very afternoon. "Let me ask you something. What about fingerprints on the knife? You can take my mine now and compare them."

"You are volunteering to do that?" he asked.

"You bet I am," I answered.

Manny made a face. "*If* prints were taken they're not in the file."

"How is that possible?" I asked.

"Kennedy was shot that week. Most of the cops were Irish then. No one did his job without his mind on the assassination. I am figuring even if prints were taken they were lost."

I understood. Though I was just a kid then, I remember how it shook everyone. I also noticed how Manny seemed to ease up a little. "Who do *you* think killed her?" he asked.

"I have no idea," I answered, but then I remembered something my father once told me. "My father said that they had enemies."

"Who had enemies?"

"Not my aunt as much as her husband, Frank. But he was in jail," I told him.

"He could have had enemies. He was selling black-market gasoline stamps. He sold them for a good profit. The talk was that he had a partner but that is so long ago I can't and probably will never find out who that was. They certainly didn't have a legal contract lying around."

"Was he in jail for the gasoline stamps scam?" I asked.

"Oh yeah, they caught up with him eventually. He got five years and was about to get out when he had a fight with another inmate and got stabbed to death. Nothing related to anything but too many guys being squashed together in small cells with nothing better to do," Manny said.

He then got quiet for a moment absorbed with a thought. He then said to me, "You told Walsh you thought someone was in the room with you."

"Yes," I said feeling a shiver go up my spine suddenly back in that room all those years earlier.

"Did you *see* anyone?"

"I felt someone watching me."

Manny seemed self-conscious to me. I wondered if all detectives acted that way. There they were asking questions to complete strangers but all the time being watched by a victim or a suspect as they did. They had to perform like an actor on stage, but they didn't have the training and it made them come off self-conscious and I saw it.

He touched the file. He then sat back. "A witness called Walsh a few weeks after the murder. She said she did see someone leave the house from the side entrance the day your aunt was killed."

"A neighbor?"

"Yeah. A woman, called it in. A housewife who lived across the street saw someone leave your aunt's house from the side door. She was housecleaning waiting for her daughter to come home from school when she peaked out the window."

I knew of that side door. "What did she see?" I asked excitedly.

Manny seemed thrilled that he got my attention. He opened the file and read what was in the report verbatim. "*Longish brown hair. Medium height. Wearing a dark rain coat. In their thirties.*"

I frowned. "That was it? That was all they said?"

Manny nodded. "That was it."

With that Manny closed the file and took a deep breath. "Thanks for taking the time," he said.

"Sure," I responded. I felt uncomfortable not knowing what I was supposed to do next.

Then he asked quickly, "Neither of your parents are alive are they?"

"No. My mother passed away just a couple of years ago. My father died much earlier than that. Why do you ask?"

"I would have liked to ask them a few questions."

"Sorry," I said.

Manny perked up. "Oh, by the way, was your mother home when you got there that Tuesday afternoon?"

I thought a moment. Actually, I didn't see her when I got home but I lied. "She was home."

"How long did it take you to walk home?"

"From my aunt's house? A few minutes."

Manny was suddenly animated. "I drove to your old neighborhood the other day. I hear it really hasn't changed much in the forty or more years. Did you walk down to your house along the sidewalk past the bus stop?"

I shook my head. "No, I took a kid's route, across the lawns, through the alley and the backyards."

Now Manny nodded. "I bet you didn't see any adults walking that way."

"I didn't see anybody," I agreed. "Why did you ask if my mother was home?"

"Because she fit the description the witness gave Walsh," he answered.

I was puzzled. "What description?"

"Of the *woman* leaving the house after you left," he told me.

I sat back. "What are you talking about?"

He quoted from the report. "Long brown hair. Medium height. In their thirties. That could describe your mother, correct?"

"But you said it was a man," I told him.

"No, I didn't. I never said it was a man seen leaving the house," he responded. "I only said she saw someone leaving the house through the side door."

I was confused. I moved in my chair. I stared at him wondering if he was lying. "This neighbor saw a *woman* leave the house right after I did," I said.

He nodded silently.

"My mother was home when I got there."

"So you say."

I lowered my head on my raised hand with my arm resting on the chair. I forced myself to remember if she was home when I got there. I had a key. I let myself in. I put the envelope on the table. I went upstairs to my room. She called me for dinner when my father got home from work an hour or so later.

"Was she home?" Manny asked.

I nodded. "She was always home," I said.

"Don't lie, Mike."

"I'm not lying. She was home. Is there anything else?"

"Yes, there is something *else.*" He opened another file. "Your mother was arrested for assault in nineteen sixty-four. Is that correct?"

"She was arrested?"

"You were twelve in nineteen sixty-four. Correct?"

"Arrested?" I vaguely remembered the police coming to our door. I remember them walking my mother out of the house. I remember my father, calm but focused, telling my mother that he would *make a call.*

That was all I remembered of that day. My mother was home the next morning. She acted as if nothing had happened. She went upstairs to the bathroom, took a shower, then made me breakfast.

I never asked her about it. Only now when Lambisi brought it up did I remember it.

"She assaulted a woman named Maria Ferrari."

"Our next door neighbor."

"Correct. According to the arrest record, this Maria Ferrari accused your mother of threatening her life and smacking her."

"She attacked me."

"Your mother?"

"No, my neighbor. Marie Ferrari. I told my mother. She didn't believe me at first but then when I was attacked again she went over to see her."

"And then your mother attacked her."

"I have no idea what happened. I was twelve."

Lambisi took a deep breath. "Your mother had to know somebody."

"What do you mean?"

"It says here that the following day all charges were dropped."

"Why?"

"This Marie Ferrari refused to press charges. It says here that she changed her mind. I guess your mother knew somebody, huh?"

"Too bad she's not here. You could have asked her."

Lambisi leaned forward. "Look, you can see why I'm thinking your mother might have done something to this aunt of yours. She fit the description and she had a history. My only question is why. But then your mother had a temper it seems. The *why* might have a simple explanation."

"Anything else?" I asked.

I then got up. I didn't hear him say anything so I kept walking. I walked away from him and his desk. I walked out of the precinct and to my car feeling much like the bewildered cherub I had been all those years ago.

I never heard from Detective Lambisi again.

# 7

## 1964
## Eleven Years Old

DURING THE SPRING of that year my father bought me roller skates and I became obsessed with them. After school I would do my homework and then if there was any sunlight left I would immediately go to the back alley and roller skate. I would go up and down the asphalt alleyway and skate around and around in circles.

One afternoon our next door neighbor stepped out of her basement door and shouted at me that I was making too much noise and she wanted me to stop. That neighbor was Marie Ferrari.

She had long dark raven hair. It fell across her shoulders curly and black. She had black eyes and her lips were always fire engine red from lipstick. In her early thirties she was married to a truck driver and had three children. Sofia was my age and the others, Joey and Gina, was younger.

They didn't get out that much and sometimes, in the summer, I would see Sofia in the backyard doing gardening with her mother. But during the winter and spring months I never saw much of them.

That particular afternoon I was wearing my V neck jacket. It was the rage for kids at that time. They were fur lined and came in red, black and sky blue with a big white V down the back and it had a hood. Mine was blue.

I loved the feeling of roller skating down through the alley sometimes up the hills and sometimes down, flying passed parked cars and the yards that lined one side and the cellar doors which lined the other.

I felt someone pull my hood and with a strong tug fling me against the wall. Being on my skates I had little control and since they were behind me they could send me in any direction they wished.

I turned and saw Marie Ferrari gripping my hood. Her large dark eyes were on fire. "I had enough!" she screamed. Then she pulled my hood even tighter and I crashed to the asphalt.

Terrified, I got up and skated away from her. I had no idea what she was angry with but in time I realized it was the noise the skates made on the asphalt that probably got her to attack me.

She stood in the center of the alley way in a black sweater and the black tight fitting stretch pants she always wore just glaring at me.

I raced up the hill and was flexible enough to run up the porch steps. I rang the bell and my mother appeared.

"Mrs. Ferrari pulled my hood," I told her.

I could see my mother's vague image on the other side of the screen door. She was wearing a light blue house coat. Her soft brown eyes were wide and interested.

"What did you do?"

"I was skating."

"I told him to stop!" Maria Ferrari shouted standing to my left facing the porch from the driveway.

My mother opened the door and came out. "Why didn't you stop?"

I had no answer.

"Get inside."

I went into the house and my mother closed the door. Once inside I tried to explain myself and what had happened. My mother listened but said nothing. That would have been the end of it except several days later out of the blue my mother told me to skate in the alleyway again so I did.

I skated up and down the alley, up and down the hills right after I did my homework.

This time Maria Ferrari, again in her black sweater and her tight fitting stretch pants with her dark raven hair flowing over her shoulders, stepped out of her basement door and grabbed my hood.

Just as she leaned back to swing me around my mother stepped out from behind our basement door. She had been watching all the time.

"Get your hands off of him," she said.

Maria Ferrari let go of me. I spun around but then quickly came to a sharp stop.

What happened next I remember very well, however, I kept it from my interview with Detective Lambisi.

I was only a couple of feet away and watched as my mother stepped up to Marie Ferrari. "If you ever touch my son again I will kill you." Then she slapped her hard across her face.

The slap echoed in the small enclave created by the two story brick homes.

My mother stood her ground and didn't move until Maria Ferrari ran back into her house. My mother then took my hand and walked back into ours.

As Detective Lambisi had told me the police did come. They did arrest my mother and the next day she was home when all charges were dropped.

I'm not sure who my father saw and what was said to Maria Ferrari but never again did she ever come near me. In fact, if the both of us were outside at the same time either in the front of the house or in the backyard, she would quickly disappear. She feared being seen with me and that was something I was sure of.

# 8

## 1968
## Fifteen Years Old

MY FATHER'S OLDER BROTHER Sam was married to a woman I called my Aunt Lucy and they lived on Mott Street in Manhattan.

My Aunt Lucy was always wearing furs and large bright jewelry. She had an older brother I knew only as Uncle Johnny Balls.

One Saturday afternoon my father and I were watching *Saturday Afternoon Boxing from Madison Square Garden* on WPIX on our black and white television when I noticed my Uncle Johnny sitting in the front row facing ringside.

"Hey, Pop, there's Uncle Johnny!" I said.

My father was eating a salami sandwich on thick Italian bread like he always liked to do on a Saturday afternoon. "Yeah," he said.

I noticed that my Uncle Johnny was just sitting there stoned-face seemingly not even interested in the fight. In those days the fights were shot with a single camera placed on a ninety degree angle to the ring. So the TV viewer could see the fight with a clear view but without close-ups or changing camera angles.

My uncle was sitting directly in the center front row seat in a suit and tie with his dark plastered back and wearing his large round rimmed classes.

"He needs an alibi," my father told me.

And that was that. It was the first time I had learned something about my uncle. He was who he was and was on television in front of the cameras to make sure that the world saw him, and that included law enforcement so that he had a perfect alibi. What his alibi was for was not my business and I knew well enough not to ask.

I continued watching the fight and my father continued eating his Italian hero.

Years later I found out that my Uncle Johnny Balls worked for the Gambino crime family. He owned a piece of every night club in New York City that played live music. I figured that meant that he got a percentage of the house probably from the owner. If the owner didn't pay his club was either burned down or closed by my uncle's men.

My father liked going out with my Uncle Johnny. They would triple date. My Uncle Eddie and Aunt Lucy and my mother and father would huddle in Uncle Johnny's big white Cadillac.

If they went out on a Saturday night to dinner my Uncle would bring along his wife Antoinette. If they went out on a Friday, he would bring along his girlfriend who was also named Antoinette.

Antoinette the girlfriend was a singer and that's how he met her. My mother once told me that she was happy that both were named Antoinette making it easier for her to never slip up and call either one of them the wrong name.

My Uncle Johnny also owned his own restaurant on Canal Street on the border of Little Italy and Chinatown. His place was called Sammy Chans. It served Chinese food and yet every Easter Sunday in the sixties we went there for dinner. Instead of eating Italian food we had Chinese food and no one complained.

The interesting thing about the restaurant was that the windows were darkened out so you couldn't look in. I figured that kept the police from taking photographs of anyone in the restaurant. Also, once inside you found yourself face to face with five foot high plastic ivy. The ivy was placed in such a way that once you entered the restaurant you couldn't find your way to any table without someone guiding you.

The tables, which were only a handful, were hidden by the ivy and could seat a half a dozen people at round tables. When we were there the place was always empty and it occurred to me that it really wasn't a business but a front for my uncle to have his meetings and the maze of plastic ivy was placed there to protect him. If anyone wanted to shoot my uncle they would never be able to find him in that restaurant. They would be stopped by the impenetrable maze and shot down by his bodyguards.

My uncle had several bodyguards. They were stout, round men in suits with flat noses, broad faces and piercing eyes. They never spoke and never left his side.

Once at my uncle's mansion in suburban Jersey outside Jersey City I remember we were invited there for a summer party.

Our cars were parked by valet parkers and then we were greeted at the door by a single bodyguard in a black suit. Despite the summer heat he wore his suit jacket. "He's carrying," father whispered to me as we entered the house.

Once inside we entered an enclave where there was a six foot statue of the Blessed Virgin Mary with her arms out protecting the world and delivering us from evil.

We were then greeted by two large black Doberman pinschers tied to posts at the front door. We then were taken out to the backyard where there was a swimming pool and a water fountain.

A pug nosed bodyguard was grilling hotdogs and hamburgers on a grill in his white shirt and black slacks and tie and eventually we were expected to enjoy ourselves despite the fact that I felt we were in a fortress.

Later that afternoon I was asked to see my Uncle Johnny in his den. I was led there by one of his bodyguards and was asked to sit in a chair facing my uncle who was sitting behind a very wide table. On it were photographs of his wife and children along with religious pictures of Jesus Christ and the Blessed Virgin.

Despite it being summer, and even though there was air conditioning, he was wearing a lemon colored suit and pristine white shirt open at the neck. He was reading something so I got to watch him. He wore a large gold chain tucked inside his shirt and he had on his wrist a gold watch that dazzled me and a large sapphire ring.

Eventually he looked up at me and smiled. His small eyes were hazel but a hazel so light colored they looked blue.

"How's the roller skating?" he asked.

"It's good. I don't roller skate as much as I used to. I like to roller skate mostly down the park with friends."

"You used to roller skate behind your house."

"Yes."

"But not anymore?"

"Not much."

He leaned in and I could smell his cologne. "You roller skate where ever you want. You want to go out for a nice roller skate at two in the morning, you go. You understand?"

"Yes."

"Nobody tells you where or when you can roller skate." He leaned back in this large wooden chair that crackled as he did. "Your mother, she is a special woman."

"Yes."

"We look out for one another, understand?"

"I do."

"Good."

Then he did something that I thought was unusual then and to this day when I remember it. He leaned his left hand on the desk and then brushed back his hair. When he was done he rested his head in his hand after placing it on the desk to lean on. He then made the sign of the cross and when he was done he made a fist with his right hand kissed it. He then looked up.

"That was a prayer."

I didn't say anything.

"I pray for the dead."

He searched my eyes. "You found her."

I knew what he was talking about.

"It was sad that you found her."

"My Aunt Josie?"

"Yes."

I didn't move.

"I loved her once."

For the first time I noticed heavy bags and dark circles under his eyes.

"You're old enough to understand. Or maybe not. A man falls in love with a woman and they marry. That was your Aunt Josie and me. When we were young though. Just teenagers."

"You didn't marry my aunt?"

"No. She met Frank. Your Uncle Frank. At first it bothered me but then in time I knew I wasn't ready for that with her. It was better he married her and not me."

It was all so confusing.

"Your Uncle Frank had troubles. Then she had troubles. She changed a lot from when I had those feelings for her. It's awful she died that way. You can't figure life. Accept that and you'll be okay."

I pretended to understand.

That was the last and only conversation I ever had with him. Several years later he disappeared. My mother had told me that one day he left his New Jersey mansion in the morning and never came home.

My father once told me that the mobster Paul Castalano never liked my Uncle Johnny and that it was when he was made head of the Gambino family he *made* my uncle disappear.

His wife found a drawer in his den and learned that my uncle Johnny Balls left behind a will. My mother told me this one day. I can't remember why. I might have asked her about him.

It seemed that not long after he disappeared and his wife Antoinette called her crying on the phone. She told my mother that she gave the papers she had found to an attorney and found that Jonny owned a hospital in Saint Louis and had several large farms in Ottawa, Canada.

They never found his body and he never wrote his wife or his children.

Looking back I am sure though that he was who Detective Lambisi was eluding to in that one and only interview. I realized that my uncle had sent someone to talk to Marie Ferrari and that was why I could roller skate in the alley anytime I wanted to. No one could tell me otherwise.

# 9

## 1973
## Twenty Years Old

I WON A POETRY CONTEST my sophomore year and was made Literary Editor of the campus magazine.

I went to school every day on my motorcycle and wore a dungaree jacket with NADA written on the front in black magic marker and an upside down cross on the back. Inspired by the use of the Spanish *nada* meaning nothing when I read it in a short story by Hemingway titled "A Clean, Well-Lighted Place."

I was lean and attractive with a hungry look in my eyes and hair that hung over my shoulders. And yet I felt the angst that comes with too much intelligence in someone not yet a complete adult.

I was lonely and tortured with the pain of directionless aspiration and confused by what path to take because I didn't have a road map.

I wanted to be a poet in the worst way. I read all I could of Byron, Keats and Shelly's poetry. I also read all I could find on their lives. I liked Keats' poetry the most but dreamed of being Lord Byron.

I adored Byron because he lived the lifestyle of a rock star and since I was not musically inclined I could only enjoy the rock groups of the 1970s while writing my own heartfelt verse.

I had nothing in common with these English Romantic poets other than identifying with their lifestyle of live fast, die young and leave a good-looking corpse. Looking back it was their passion for language and emotion that drew me to them.

I admired Keats and mused over his short life and his intense love affair with the even younger Fanny Brawne. His poem "This Living Hand" floored me. In the short blank verse a vampire-like poet accused his lover of indifference after his death and he wanted none of it. He wanted her to take his hand as it came to her from the grave and her blood would pour into him. The tone of the poem is about the immortality of love and that notion thrilled me.

Shelly rounded off the three greats for me, even though I wasn't a fan. I'd like to have met his wife, Mary, in some fantasy world.

When I won the poetry contest the judge was the head of the Modern Foreign Language Department. He was the enigmatic Dr. Ianucci.

He was a petite man with an eccentric way of using eye liner to bring attention to his large violet eyes. He also dressed in very expensive suits and excellent stylish ties and with exquisite features.

After I won the contest he invited me up to his office and offered me as much time as I wanted to spend with him. So it came about that every Thursday around four o'clock I'd go up to his office in Bent Hall. When I showed up he'd tell his secretary to close the door. We would share hours together in his plush office which was filled with books as he sat behind his enormous wooden desk recommending what poets I should read.

He recommended Andre Gide, Rilke and the Italian poet Montale. I would find the books in the universities extensive libraries and we would then discuss what I had read.

Some days Dr. Ianucci and I would sit and talk into the early evening. He'd drawn the blinds and time would just stop and neither of us would care.

It was the poet Rilke I found the most engrossing. His famous last lines of the poem "Archaic Torso of Apollo" stunned me. They are "...for there is no place / that does not see you. / You must change your life."

After reading that poem and coming to the last line I realized that I found my mantra. I had to change my life. I was now sure of it more than ever before. I decided then and there that even though I had no examples to follow, no roads to travel down I was going to dedicate my life to writing and capturing my feelings. Those feelings might be in the form of plays or novels or even poetry.

I wasn't going to take a working class job or pursue higher education so that I could teach. I was going to *do* and become a writer or better yet a poet. A living breathing poet, I was going to dedicate my life to that mission.

I wasn't sure how I was going to make the change but it was now a necessity and I spoke about this every time I was in Dr. Ianucci's company.

I implored myself, if that was possible, not to fall prey to the mundane but to allow myself to dream— but to dream wisely. "Oh my soul, do not aspire to Immortal life / but exhaust the limits of the possible."

I found Pindar through Camus and I found Camus in the library by accident. I was searching through the aisles looking for something to read when I came across Camus' *The Stranger*. Reading that novel shattered my life. The elegance of the simple phrasing staggered me. A man knowing nothing about his life moving through it without emotion and without reflection startled and haunted me.

I knew only a little then and learned much later on that I was a passenger in my own life. I was haunted by this insight and though still so very young reading *The Stranger* gave me a vision into my future.

I searched for everything he wrote and in some essay I found I read Pindar's quote and was on my way to exhaust the limits of the possible.

Aside from afternoons, Dr. Ianucci invited me to his apartment in Manhattan for dinner. We had these dinners once every couple of months.

He was a fascinating literary man who believed in the magnitude of poetry for the soul. He also believed firmly and without doubt that it was suffering that formed greatness in poets.

He was from a working class family in Pittsburg of all places. He was not only eccentric and highly stylized and intellectual he was clearly asexual. Of course in meeting him you would believe he was gay but he never talked about sex or its importance in his life.

He never approached me about it, not in conversation or in action. If he ever had a lover of either gender he never spoke about them. He never married or had any children and lived for his career in academia.

His apartment in Manhattan was elegant and it was the first doorman apartment I had ever been in. He had a wonderful chandelier in his dining room and we would share a bottle of scotch and have delightful meals I can only slightly recall.

Sometimes he'd take me to a local restaurant in his neighborhood of Park Avenue in the Seventies and after we spent hours talking about poetry and my life we'd retreat to his place and spend more time there talking about poetry and my life.

We spent most of the time talking about loneliness and my feelings for Christine; and the importance of my suffering.

When I told him I wanted to be a writer though other than being a poet I wasn't sure what kind of writing I'd do, he told me that I should consider a menial job. The more menial the more I could use the frustration from suffering to fuel my poetic soul. He wanted me to dig ditches during the day and pour my agony into poetry during the night.

I found the notion painful to accept. We never argued about it but it was there all the time under the surface of my inner life: to be an artist first and foremost or to actually have a life with pleasure and prosperity.

"You were given a gift, Michael, a gift," he told me one night.

"It is a gift then?" I asked.

"Given to you."

"Who gave it to me?" I asked.

"You could believe it was given by God. You could believe it was an accident of birth. You could believe that some greater power in the universe has chosen you to share your emotional experiences with those who need to read it so that it comforts them because they see that someone else has felt the same way. Some stranger who they may never meet in person has undergone the same loss and this helps them get through it."

"Is that what a poet is?"

He smiled. "I read your poetry to help me through my own loneliness."

I nodded shyly.

"You have a responsibility. You have a mission. You can't turn away from it. Everything else in your life is secondary. Who you love, who you hate. They all take second place to what you must write. You must write poems to share. You must share your feelings, your sensations, your thoughts, your fears, your desires with the world. That is not only a responsibility but also a duty."

I squirmed in my chair. Up to that point I had no intention of making my love of words a duty as he stated it was going to be. Even though he was talking about himself I knew he was taking about my obligation to my vocation.

He leaned back. "This is why we are friends. Not for any other reason you might think but I am in your life only to read about what you fear, miss, long for and nothing else so that I might comfort my own loneliness with your poetry."

~ ~ ~

It was fascinating how much Christine and Dr. Ianucci reminded me of one another. Of course, in the most general of descriptions they were as different as night and day. He was a middle-aged man and she was a young woman. He was an extraordinary academic and she was a vibrant working class woman. He was asexual and she was entirely sexual.

There were some other similarities these two people shared. They both had large violet eyes and had birthdays on the same day.

They both seemed otherworldly and mystical. I hadn't learned that side of Christine at this time but eventually it came to me when I did get involved with her. They also shared a fragility that perhaps appealed to the poet in me. They both hung onto the ephemeral in life as if it were made of concrete. Both lives would end sadly.

They were so much alike in their souls it perplexed me as if it were some unwritten destiny that both would be in my life at the same time.

It was also my conversations with Dr. Ianucci which propelled me a few years later to pursue Christine after her marriage to Louis Jr. fell apart.

~ ~ ~

I also shared my Aunt Josie's death with Dr. Ianucci in ways I didn't share it with anyone else.

"That must have had a profound effect on you, Michael," he said.

"I'm not sure of the effect it had on me," I replied.

"It may have made you the poet you are becoming. You were so young when it happened."

"What do you think was in the envelope?" I'd ask him.

"A family secret. All families have them," he said softly.

"I supposed they do."

"I imagine the envelope had something to do with you. You need to accept that about your life," he said.

"Accept what?" I asked.

"Accept that there is something about yourself you are in denial of. We all do that to ourselves. Most of us can look away while others embrace the mystery. I suggest you embrace the mystery," he said. "Or you will suffer from not knowing. Or you may suffer from *knowing*."

I grew close to Dr. Ianucci over the following few years. Eventually he asked me to invite others to his apartment for his salon.

I brought painters and other poets from the college and our conversations were the kind you only have once in your life. I imagine anyone who pursues a craft of some kind, one that involves abstract thinking or a passion for whatever the craft is, has experiences like we had.

One night I looked around the room and saw how young and attractive we were and what energy we had. It was at one of these salons that I realized I had something special, a gift for storytelling.

Yes, I considered myself a poet but I was also a storyteller and the two needs struggled to come to life inside me.

If it were up to Doctor Ianucci I'd be a poet and nothing else. Not an academic or a novelist or film maker.

He was the reason I got into the Columbia master's program to truly study literature. He made the introductions for me to their graduate school. He wrote my letter of recommendation.

It was after I graduated Columbia that I saw him for the last time. He had lost his position as the Chair of the department through political intrigue and it devastated him.

He could no longer afford his elegant apartment and throw his faculty dinner parties. Perhaps someone got jealous of him flaunting his stylish ways but in the end it didn't matter. His demotion made him so sad he decided to retire and move back to Pittsburg.

I lost touch with him right before he moved.

# 10

## 1988
## Thirty-Five Years Old

I ONCE ASKED MY FATHER what was in the white envelope. It was only days after he was diagnosed with liver cancer. He was frightened and only sixty-nine years old.

I didn't know much about liver cancer then and how deadly it was. Being thirty-five and adrift spending my time traveling and struggling to make a living writing some nights to lose myself I did cocaine and hung out with several wannabe gangsters like Louie Jr. I was also going from one woman to another not really sure what I was searching for.

My father had gone in for a routine checkup when they found spots on his liver and there were too many to try and surgically remove. He was facing chemotherapy and radiation the following week.

He wanted to talk to me about taking care of my mother before he was in a weakened state so he asked me to take a walk around the neighborhood.

Once I had become an adult we spent very little time speaking to one another. I was busy being lost and he was busy planning his retirement.

He wasn't happy with the direction my life had taken. He was disappointed I hadn't married and had children. He thought I might be gay and said so several times to me.

When I was much younger and we were at a party he'd make me dance with women. I felt so self conscious that I'd sometimes become completely immobile and my inability to socialize embarrassed him.

I wasn't entirely the cherub when he did that but I was still a little man half boy and half teenager. The only time he did get impressed with me was when I learned the twist. I played the record over and over again in the house so he could watch me dance it. Often when my female cousins came over we would dance the twist time and time again. I see now that it was when watching me dance that he could see I was taking after him.

My father grew up on Mott Street in what they called Little Italy in Manhattan and he loved to dance. He was the youngest of seven children and told me only one story about his father over and over again.

It was when his father had a stroke and someone had to take care of him. So he was the youngest of the siblings who wasn't yet working who would shave the paralyzed man when he could.

"I'd shave my father every day," he'd tell me. "He'd sit in the chair and I would put on the soap and then get the razor. I was only a kid but it was my job in the family to shave him."

I didn't like hearing that story. I wasn't sure if he was telling me that he expected me to do that for him if he became unable to move.

My father never graduated grammar school and was not allowed to go into the army during World War II because when he was a kid he fell off a tenement roof top and damaged both his feet.

The one story I did like hearing over and over again was the one where he met my mother. It seems my father was a serial dater and loved to date as many women at one time as he could.

He was at a wedding one summer night in Brooklyn and met my mother. However, the wedding was nearly over. He gave the band leader a couple of dollars to play one last song so he could ask my mother to dance. Yet even before he did that, he went to ask my grandfather for permission.

My grandfather Mike, a hard man with a solid physical presence and a bad right arm stricken from a stroke he suffered.

I heard that once he nearly killed a man with a single punch to the head. It seemed he was standing on the corner with some friends and the man cursed in front of a woman. My grandfather hit him so hard he was rushed to the hospital. If the man had died he would have been arrested for murder. His cousins by marriage were cops and they hid him until the man recovered.

Well, the night my father approached him he allowed my father to ask my mother to dance and they did. After the song was over my father asked for my mother's phone number and she gave it to him.

My father called my mother several times asking to see her and every time he called she told her parents to tell my father she was out.

My mother liked to go out with her girlfriends and according to her telling of it she wasn't looking for any kind of romance especially with this tall, lanky dark haired man who seemed full of himself because he was from Manhattan.

She came from a big extended family in Williamsburg, Brooklyn on Lorimer and Richardson streets right off the corner of McCarren Park. Two of her uncles, Sunny and Louie were New York City policemen and owned the building.

She lived on the top floor with her parents and her younger brother my Uncle Carmine.

Well, as the story goes, my father never gave up and continued calling my mother and eventually they went on a date and that date turned into another.

My mother continued to resist but it seemed my father's persistence paid off. Years after they both died I was going through their things in the old house and I found several love letters my father wrote to my mother. He was a clerk at the Universal International Film Warehouses on Eleventh Avenue so the love letters were written on Universal Movies' letter head. They were meticulously written describing his day and how he looked forward to her call and their date that weekend.

It was clear he had a deep affection for her so evident that in some of the letters he would write that when they spoke he couldn't reveal how much he felt about her because his boss was standing right beside him. He would write how he longed for the sound of her voice. In all the letters he would sign at the bottom *Love Ed.*

I only found one letter my mother wrote to him. Only one letter she saved. The letter filled only half a page. It read, "I love you, I love you, I love you, I love you, I love you, I love you, I love you."

Our walk that afternoon lasted longer than I expected. My father was very thin his whole life and it was unusual but he was diagnosed with type 2 diabetes when he reached middle-age.

Walking beside him I had forgotten how thin he was. He also wore a toupee. He went bald when he was in his early forties and sometime after that he decided he needed to wear one. He came home one day with it showing my mother and me and I was incredulous but he felt it made him look younger.

As we took our strides I could see his tiny hazel eyes in the sunlight and his thin angular face aimed directly ahead as we walked and talked. I knew he wasn't long for this life then but like I said I was oblivious to the inevitable outcome of such a disease.

I tried to imagine what I looked like to him, his only son with my dark trimmed beard and longish hair. I always felt that the cherub never left my face and I looked too sweet and innocent for an adult in the cutthroat world. I found myself in a beard which gave me some gravitas.

During our walk together my father told me that he had read my poetry and some of my fiction and thought it was *cold*. He told me that if he were a writer his writing would be *warm*.

I wasn't sure what he meant at all though I thought perhaps he meant his work would be less abstract than mine. I found some pages he had written. He tried a novel once dictating it to my mother.

My mother carefully wrote what he had written in her excellent Catholic school handwriting. It added up to seven yellow pages of paper he probably got from a pad out of the warehouse.

I couldn't follow what he wrote but I was told he quit being a writer because I was born. I also learned from his older brother Sam that my father worked beside another clerk who wrote a potboiler novel and when it became a bestseller he quit being a clerk. I believe that was why my father tried his hand at fiction. He had dreams of writing a best seller about five friends growing up on Mott Street.

My father was a terrific Cha-cha-cha dancer and came up with a move where he would stamp his right foot. He would lean in and swing my mother around and watch her with glee. His face beamed with joy when he danced and especially when he danced with her.

Though he lost all his hair by the time he was in his early forties, when he was a teenager he wore his thick black hair slicked up high and though he went to work in a warehouse as a clerk and made sure he always wore a suit and tie to the job.

I would watch him walk proudly to the bus stop on the corner in his suit and tie realizing that he wanted his small world to know that he was a professional and he was a respected working man. Not long before he died I found out that he never made more than fifteen thousand dollars a year. It amazed me that he accomplished so much on so little.

When I was a kid he told me that he belonged to several dance clubs in the West Village. He was such a great dancer they all wanted him to belong to their club because his dancing attracted all the women.

There were a few things I remembered about my father when I was young. One was when I was not even six or seven I told my mother that I thought my father wasn't interested in my feelings. I was the cherub in full bloom then. I can see myself sitting on the sofa facing my mother relaying to her that I was not happy with how he ignored how I felt about things.

My mother shared  this with my father who when he got home. Taking off his fedora and raincoat he confronted me.

"What's wrong with you?"

"You don't care how I feel."

"You are always talking about your feelings," he told me.

Looking back I realized that I wasn't the normal little boy. I was sensitive, perhaps too sensitive.

Two times I recall my father was my hero. I was playing baseball in the local Catholic school league and one of the premiere players was bullying me. His father was the coach and I never got to play because of that.

Hearing this, my father came down Saturday afternoons to the park to hit batting practice and stood in the dugout making sure I played.

I got my big chance in the last inning of the very last game. The coach's son was pitching a shutout and no one player on the opposing team had hit a ball in the outfield.

Though we were ahead one to zero the coach's son had walked the bases loaded and with two outs, as if a slap in the face, I was placed in center field. I imagine the coach figured no one would hit the ball out to me. Well with the count three balls and two strikes the opposing batter hit a line drive straight at me.

I ran in to catch it. I could feel all eyes in that small ball field were on me. I saw the ball scream out of the clouds nothing more than a white dot in an ocean of blue and white.

I ran for it and as I did my baseball cap flew over my head. For some absurd reason, perhaps to look good doing it, I continued to run towards the sinking baseball reaching my glove hand out for the ball and using my free right hand to sit my hat back on my head.

The ball fell right into my glove and the game was over. I trotted back to my team and instead of cheers for my unexpected winning play in center field all I heard was, "Why did he worry about his hat?"

The other time he was my hero was when I developed a kidney disease. I was eleven years old and was placed in a hospital for tests. My time there grew from one week to two with no sign of me being released by Christmas.

I remember being in the children's ward watching each young child be brought in and some being let out as I counted down the days to the holiday.

I became fascinated with a pretty dark haired nurse who came in every morning to give me a sponge bath. She had big brown serious eyes and a womanly figure. I never said a word to her but I couldn't take my eyes off her face and her hands as she kept me clean.

I developed a crush on her and I was too shy to even speak to her. I was severely disappointed when she didn't show up one morning. I heard from the other nurses that she had been reassigned to another ward.

One night when all the lights were out my father appeared in the glow of a dim light coming from the street. He was holding a bag with a burger and fries.

He walked towards me with a broad grin and wildness in his eyes I had never seen before. I had told my mother that I didn't like the food in the hospital so he brought me a delicious burger from White Castle, I was ecstatic with joy.

I had never seen my father so vital and alive in his leather jacket and collar up with his natural dark wavy hair that he still possessed then blown array from the wind outside.

He had to tell me several times how he gave the security guards the slip making his way up to the children's ward then charmed the nurse on duty by telling her he wanted to see his son.

He was proud of himself for eluding the security guard and making it all the way up to the children's ward in the middle of the night with my bounty. When he reached me he had a joy in his eyes proud and clearly excited by the success of his adventure.

"I walked past the security guard when he was looking the other way. I raced into the elevator without a pass," he said his grand smile beaming in the shadows around us.

As soon as he handed me the burger I devoured it and the fries.

"I don't have much time. The nurse saw me when I came into your ward and told me I have five minutes. But I had to see you."

In my entire life I don't think I ever saw him that happy or thrilled as he was that night.

I had another memory I never shared with him again. It was a Sunday morning and he was sitting in the living room having coffee with his friend Joe, *the cop*.

Joe was my father's friend from Mott Street and still lived there with his wife Trudy. They were having a conversation when my father handed me a quarter and asked me to go to the store on the Plateau to pick up the Sunday newspaper.

I was probably no more than eight years old and I put on my bulky winter coat and made the walk up in the sunshine and bought the heavy Sunday paper. There was a strong wind blowing and though I was bundled up I could feel it but I liked doing my father a favor and getting his newspaper for him.

On the way down the hill two older guys approached me. They asked me for money but I had none to give so they punched me several times in the stomach. I fell to my knees and the newspaper that I had desperately held slipped through my fingers and flew out of my hands and up into the wind.

I took their blows in complete silence in the bright sunshine on my knees on the grass along the bus stop. The truth is that my jacket was so thick I hardly felt anything. I guess the way I took the blows stoically and without a sound made them stop, turn and run off.

I went back and told my father what happened. The two men raced out of the house looking for the two thugs but came back without finding them.

~ ~ ~

In our walk my father and I made our way up the same hill to the Plateau and passed by my Aunt Josie's house. I stopped a moment and my father stopped with me.

"Terrible thing," he said.

"Who do you think did it, Pop?" I asked. I always called him Pop.

"Josie had some enemies," he said.

"Aunt Josie had enemies? I don't believe that."

My father walked on. "From the old neighborhood. Mostly Frank's enemies and not hers."

"I wish I knew who did it," I said.

"It's the past. It doesn't mean anything now. Don't think about it. Go on with your life."

"What was in the envelope?" I asked.

He looked at me as if he had forgotten.

"The white envelope I picked up from Aunt Josie every Tuesday after I came home from school."

He didn't answer me. My father believed in protecting me. He tried his best to keep me from pain, disease, disappointment and for many years even death. His own death was the first he couldn't keep me from.

"*What* envelope?" he asked.

I wanted to remind him but I realized then and there he would deny there ever was one. He was protecting me from something and I had absolutely no power of persuasion to get him to explain it to me.

But I had to ask him one more question. Something I had learned from Christine years ago and never asked my father mainly because I didn't want to know the answer.

"Were you partners with Uncle Frank?"

He didn't react. "With Uncle Frank? What kind of partners?"

"He went to jail for selling forged gasoline stamps during War World II. I heard once that he had a partner."

My father nodded. "Oh yeah, that. There was always talk that he had a partner. I have no idea who it was. Nobody did. But we figured it was Josie's cousin. Louis Sr."

We had continued up the hill when he told me about his cancer. He was more afraid of the pain than the actual dying. His big fear was that he'd die like his father of a stroke and that his heart would give out.

Yet he didn't die like that. The cancer killed him and it took his life swiftly. He was dead within six months of that walk of ours.

"Take care of your mother," he told me. It was literarily the last thing he ever directly said to me.

I was with him the day he died and my mother cried over his bed in the hospital. "We were cheated, Ed." I heard her say.

I took her arm on the walk through the cemetery to his grave.

# 11

## 1967
## Fourteen Years Old

MY FRESHMAN YEAR in McClancy High School I was pursued by a bully. His name was Johnny Lynch. He was tall, loud and aggressive. I was no longer a cherub. By the age of thirteen I had become a boy. A boy is someone not yet a true teenager.

I was a boy and though I was ordered to wear a tie and jacket as my school uniform every day I hated pretending to dress like a businessman. I hated feeling stifled and a tie and jacket made me feel that way.

All our teachers were male. Half were lay teachers and the other half Christian Brothers, an interesting phenomenon to me. They didn't take their vows to become priest but they wore cassocks. They couldn't administer the sacraments but they were still bound by vows of obedience and celibacy.

Some were obsessed with basketball and others those out of shape, perhaps obsessed with some inner demon gnawing at them perhaps something from their past they needed to make penance for or just try and forget. Why else would they live such an extreme life? It was the only way I could justify denying themselves physical comfort and the freedom to do what they wanted.

Also unlike priests they were rough edged men who did not suffer fools easily.

The athletic, either in their twenties or even much older, were slim, clean cut and not as much interested in academics as the others.

The others were usually overweight and or heavy smokers who indulged away from everyone else and certainly never in front of the students. They probably were secret alcoholics as well.

Most of the lay teachers were easygoing, personable and in their thirties. All of them were white and male.

It was an all boys' school and like the brothers and teachers I found my classmates divided up into three general categories. There was those I was the most like. They were quiet, loners and seemingly introspective.

The next third were the highly evolved. I can't recall their names but they became future CEOs and heads of states. They were talkative, supremely confident, and well-groomed and were at the top of the class academically. They belonged to the Social Club, the History Club and the Yearbook Club. They headed every school committee and seemed to whisk in and out of class as if in limousines.

The last third were the thugs. They were loud and aggressive. Half of them weren't actually bad guys but just loose cannons who liked to talk when they shouldn't, disobey the brothers and break things when an authority figure wasn't around.

Looking back they were just rebels who had a difficult time following authority. They ranged from Jimmy Kerwin who was the leader of a pack of tough guys who spent most of their time doing scams. They'd try to steal tests from the principal's office or tell temporary teachers that there was school holidays that didn't exist and get the class to be sent home early.

They usually averaged a C and in looking back I can't believe any of them learned anything from their high school education. Mike Myles, Nicky DeFino and Jimmy Kerwin were the most notorious.

The other half of the tough guys were out and out dangerous. They'd come to school in stolen cars; mug some of the loners when they found them standing at a bus stop and in the case of Lynch, they bully those they figured were easy to bully.

Lynch began bulling me one Thursday afternoon at lunch. It was Thursday that lemon cake was served with pasta. Every boy in the school looked forward to that tasty lemon cake and for some reason Lynch decided he was going to take mine.

He'd do the same thing every *pasta* Thursday. He'd walk to my table where I was sitting and look at me. "Oh, it's Thursday Tucci. Lemon cake day," he'd say and then reach over and grab my cake off my tray.

He'd eat it in front of me and walk back to his table.

It was this time that I made friends with another loner. His name is lost to the deepest recess of my memory but I remember thinking years later that he reminded me of the actor Charlie Bronson in his look and demeanor.

I don't know how we became friends that freshman year but at recess we'd walk in the schoolyard which would remind anyone of a prison. A tall silver painted metal fence rose up from a concrete wall as if to keep the students inside the perimeter for the brothers to keep an eye on us as if we were in a jail.

The boys would break up into groups walking back and forth from the fence to the school walls.

Jimmy Kerwin and his small gang would congregate near the back wall where they'd sneak a smoke despite the constant surveillance by one of the brothers.

They also harassed the loners by asking them for money. When the loner declined they'd ridicule them which was a threat in itself.

After being victimized by Lynch for several Thursdays in a row Charlie Bronson said to me, "You have to do something, man. You can't keep letting this guy take your lemon cake. It doesn't look good."

I agreed but I had no idea how to stop Lynch since he was six feet tall. I would lie in bed at night looking up at the ceiling hoping to get some inspiration from the Mother of God the only person I prayed to in heaven since I believed in her womanly compassion not only because she was Christ's mother but because she was a mother.

I'm not sure if I got the inspiration from her or from myself but I did forge a plan and decided to try it out the following morning in school.

I approached Jimmy Kerwin and his cronies as they snuck smokes with their back to the concrete wall.

"I don't think you know who I am but I want to ask you something," I said.

To my surprise he was interested in hearing what I had to say. I explained how Lynch was taking my lemon cake every Thursday and I volunteered to do Jimmy's homework for him if he would help me out.

Jimmy quickly took me in and said. "Okay, you got a deal. So, this Thursday when Lynch takes your lunch, stab him with your fork."

I was disconcerted. That didn't sound like a plan it sounded like an act of suicide. "Then what do I do?" I asked.

"When we break for recess you come hang with us," he told me.

I walked away unable to share his dubious directions with anyone. I hardly slept the nights leading up to Thursday's lunch and the lemon cake and when Thursday morning came I shut down all emotion focusing on one thing and one thing only and that was the mission given to me by Jimmy Kerwin which would end my problem with Lynch.

All the next morning I kept still focusing on the task at hand thinking through every detail and when we were excused for lunch I went to the cafeteria took my tray and found my friend Charlie Bronson and sat next to him.

Half way through my meal, just like clockwork I saw Lynch walking toward my table. Without me prompting him Charlie Bronson, who was not privy to my plan, blurted out "Here he comes."

I looked up and there he was with his big grin and short cropped hair cut and light blue eyes gleaming as he looked down on me. "Oh, Tucci, it's Thursday. Hmm, lemon cake," he said placing his voice in a high register as if I was his Valentine's Day sweetheart and he was wooing me. He reached his hand out to my tray.

Just as he was about to grab my lemon cake I picked up my fork, held it tightly, and jabbed him right above his right knuckle.

Lynch shouted in pain like a dog hit by a car and got Brother Robert's attention who was sitting eating his lunch on the other side of the cafeteria.

Lynch grabbed his hand lowered his jaw to me and muttered loud enough for me to hear. "You are *dead*." He then rushed back to his table.

"He's going to kill you," Charlie Bronson said.

"I know," I answered.

As soon as recess came I raced out of the cafeteria searching the schoolyard for Kerwin.

As I moved through the meandering students I saw Lynch pushing others as he flew towards me.

I found Kerwin and the gang and raced over to him. "I did what you said to do, Jimmy."

"What did I tell you to do?" he asked.

I frowned. "When he reached for my lemon cake I stabbed him with my fork."

"You did *that*?" he asked.

I nodded. Just then Lynch reached me. I turned and saw him glare.

I didn't even have a chance to turn to Kerwin when I heard him say. "Hey, Lynch, Mike Tucci is with us. So beat it."

As Kerwin said that both Mike Myles and Nicky DeFino made a human wall and I slipped behind it.

Lynch was mystified as he absorbed the new information. Then, without saying a word, he turned and slinked back into the oblivious crowd.

After that day I never had another problem with Lynch. I did find out that he dropped out of school and then got drafted and was sent to Vietnam.

There was one thing that happened one night I will always recall. Jimmy and Mike Myles asked me to hang out with them so I did.

They went to a park in Astoria right after school to meet their girlfriends and told me they had a girl for me named Maria.

I can still see the autumn leaves filling the sidewalk, the brisk chilly air flowing through the night and the rays of light falling with a bright amber color across the park bench we were sitting on.

Jimmy and Mike smoked cigarettes, drank whiskey from a flask and kissed their girlfriends while I sat on the park bench like a cherub next to Maria.

She was still wearing her catholic school uniform and sat with perfect posture watching with curiosity as the others made out. We exchanged looks but I could hardly say a word to her I was frozen with shyness. I was immobile because I didn't know what was expected of me. I wasn't Jimmy or Mike and the only thing I wanted to do was go home.

"She's leaving you," Mike said to me.

"You can't let her do that to you," Jimmy chimed in.

I turned and saw Maria walking away from me.

"Be a man," Mike said.

"Yeah, get your woman," Jimmy shot at me.

I suppose the soon to emerge confident teenager was in his early stages of development because all at once I felt some life force take over my being.

It kicked away the cherub and without explanation jumped up from the bench and rushed over to Maria.

"Where you going?" I said but it sounded more like a demand than a question.

"Home," she said uttering the only words she said to me so far and eventually the entire night.

With that I pushed her back up against the park fence and kissed her strongly on the lips. She was the first girl I had ever kissed and though the action looked violent it wasn't. I was so awkward in my physicality I just managed not to fall when I pushed her.

I could feel her lips pushing against mine and her hair blowing in my face. I felt her tongue searching for mine and her arms around my shoulders.

We had so much clothing on I couldn't feel her body but I could smell her freshly washed hair and taste the wetness of her lips and along with the night blowing across my face it all felt so primitive and alive.

We kissed standing up against the fence for a long time and later we sat on the bench kissing some more and we were both so enthralled by the physical mysteries of one another's bodies we hadn't realized that the others had left us alone.

We sat kissing as if the night didn't have a clock. I was unable to free myself from the sensuality of her hair and her lips and our silent communication was enticing beyond words.

Eventually I walked her to her bus in silence and waited for mine impatiently telling my parents when I got home that I was with a study group and I was exhausted so I was going straight to bed.

~ ~ ~

I didn't see Jimmy and Mike again until our thirtieth high school reunion. We were in the school auditorium and we shook hands like long lost comrades.

The first thing he told me was that he wanted to thank me for something I did for him back in senior year. I reminded him how much I need to thank him but surprisingly he had forgotten how he helped me with Lynch and I had forgotten how I helped him.

It seems I helped him cheat on a true or false English quiz. However, Jimmy got too many questions right by changing some of my answers so he wouldn't look to smart. The problem was that he unknowingly changed the ones I had wrong and he scored a ninety-six when I got the second highest grade in class with a ninety-two.

Of course, he was taken into the principal's office and since they couldn't prove that he cheated they gave him another test right there on the spot and he managed to pass with seventy-two.

I realized looking back that I had no trouble making friends with someone who was trouble and I had no problem lying. Lying had become part of my DNA ever since my parents told me to lie to Detective Walsh.

Yet I didn't see it as lying. I saw it as keeping the truth a secret.

# 12

## 1974
## Twenty-One Years Old

IT WAS A WARM NIGHT and I stood naked at her window looking out into the night. I was watching an abandoned compact car on fire burning on a side street alongside McCarren Park. I was filled with disgust since neither police cars or fire trucks had responded. From where I stood five stories up and a block away I could see a Latino teenage gang dancing around the fire.

It was Brooklyn in the seventies and the police didn't care. To them it was a harmless fire burning in a neighborhood plagued by drugs and violence.

I turned to the left looking down at my own Volkswagen Bug making sure it was untouched.

It was in the days of major crime in New York City. It was when the police only responded to serious crime and not quality of life crimes like they started to do under Guiliani.

In those days homicides were rising each month and the police had the policy of only responding to a felony and not preventing it.

Now they call it stop-and-frisk and that badly named policy turned the city around from a crime ridden one to one where a criminal could never let their guard down.

If they jumped a turnstile and had a gun in their pocket they would be frisked. The cop would run their name through the computer to see if they had outstanding warrants. Most did and were sent back to jail.

But in those days before Braxton and Marples, the two police detectives who came up with the plan and proposed it to then Mayor Guiliani, the city was worse than the Wild West. There was no law and order.

"It makes me sick," I said turning back to the fire.

"Nobody cares about here," I heard Christine tell me. "Why do you let it bother you?"

"The city is falling apart and nobody is doing anything about it," I answered.

"People have given up on it," Christine said.

"I don't give up on things that matter to me," I told her.

"You're talking about me as well, aren't you?"

I turned to her. The room was lit only by the ray of light from a street lamp coming through her bedroom window.

Christine was naked facing me as she lay on her right side on the bed. We had just made love and her womanly shape drew me to her. Everything about her was overwhelming; her femaleness, her large bewitching eyes, her breasts and her smooth nearly perfectly formed hips and belly. She offered it all to me and I was a glutton petrified that one day it all might be taken from me.

I walked over, lie down beside her and put my head against the pillow so that she could rest her head on my chest.

"You know I am—" I answered.

"You think too much about things," she said.

I put my right hand on her hip slipping it down over her bottom. I left it there as if keeping my hand pressed against her flesh would make the sensuous experience a part of me.

"I think just this moment I realize how much you really like and care for me," she said.

I wasn't mature enough to smile at such a comment. Being a young man I was serious about everything or at least the most important things like romantic love, death, the future.

When I didn't answer she looked up at me. I could see her face in the line of soft light and said, "You know I do."

I wish I could say that all love was just physical attraction. I wish I could say that it was her breasts I wanted in my mouth, her ass in my hands and her mouth on my penis and it would all make sense. That way all emotions between us could be explained by biology and carnal desire.

Yet with Christine there was something mystical and spiritual about our coupling. When I slept at her apartment I'd wake up sensing someone else in the room. I'd feel someone watching me like I did that afternoon in my Aunt Josie's living room.

With Christine I felt as if I was being embraced by the unseen. I wasn't sure what it was that made me feel that there was some kind of destiny between us, some plan put in action that neither one of us had created.

I wondered sometimes if it were her beauty alone that drew me to her. And was she drawn to me by her knowledge of my childhood tragedy?

Married to Louis Jr. for only a year and a half she and I started seeing one another immediately when she called me to tell me she had left him.

He was thrown into desperate straits by her leaving. He did drugs and lost a considerable amount of weight until his father had him put in a hospital to recover.

Nothing however, would bring Christine back to him. She told me that it was a mistake and she knew it on her wedding day and that she wished she only had the courage not to show up at the altar that morning.

Now, she was barely surviving and working as a secretary in a Manhattan law firm and living in a scary part of Williamsburg but it was part of her plan to change her life.

I had read her the Rilke poem sometime when we first met and realized lying in bed that night that she had taken those words to heart consciously or subconsciously and it was because of me.

"I know you don't like to talk about it but one night Louis Jr. said to me that he thinks he knows who killed your aunt," she told me in a whisper.

I stayed silent.

"Frank, her husband, illegally sold gas rationing stamps that they used during World War II and made a lot of money from them. Louis said that he had a partner but cheated him. And that partner wanted to get even. But since Frank was in jail for that other thing he did, his partner decided to take his revenge by killing Frank's wife."

"I never hear that before," I said. "Who was his partner?"

She pulled away from me.

"What's wrong? Why can't you tell me who it was?" I asked.

"I shouldn't be telling you because it's all just talk. Louis Jr. made me swear never to tell you," she said.

"Why not tell me?" I asked.

She moved to the other side of the bed and stood up. She put on a T-shirt from the chair, pulled it up and over her head and put it on. It barely covered her bottom.

She went into the kitchen and put on the light. I could see her from the bed since there was no wall between the rooms.

I watched her find her wine glass from earlier and seeing that some wine was left she sipped it. She sat on a wooden chair, the only one in the small apartment, and faced me. "Your father," she said.

I sat up. "What?"

"You never knew?"

"That's crazy," I told her. Now I got up off the bed and walked over to her.

I labored with the notion. "If that's true, tell me, what was in the envelope I collected every Tuesday?"

"What envelope?" she asked.

I explained to her realizing that she didn't know anything about it.

As I told her about my chore I saw her light up and I thought the same thing at the same time. "It was a payoff perhaps. Money was in the envelope," I said.

"Was the envelop thick?" she asked.

I could feel it in my hand. "It could have been hundreds. Pressed together they wouldn't feel like a lot but back then that was a lot of money."

I didn't want to talk about it anymore and I told Christine. She understood. We got back to bed and tried to sleep she drifted off but I couldn't, instead I thought about where my life was going and didn't want to think where it had been.

I wanted to embrace the future and turn my back on the past. I didn't want to care about where I was from at all. I wanted to create who I was *going* to be.

I was young and didn't realize how foolish a notion that was. I didn't realize then that no matter whom I thought I was going to change myself into, I was always going to be who I was. Change was impossible.

Somewhere in the middle of the night when I saw that she was awake I took Christine's hand.

"What?" she asked.

"I want to marry you," I said. "I want to have children with you. I feel close to you like no one else."

She let go of my hand and said, "I can't do that."

"Why not?" I asked.

"I need someone to take care of me," she answered. "I could never marry a poet."

"That's a crazy thing to say," I told her.

She tiled her face to me. "You don't love *me*. You love my body."

"Christine, tell me the truth. Why wouldn't you marry me?"

She took her time and touched my face. "There's something tragic about you, Michael, and I have been there before. My husband was like you. I don't want to spend my time with another tragic man."

We didn't talk the rest of the night. I left the next morning while she was asleep. Since it was warm she was only slightly covered by the blanket.

The morning light lit her from behind. Her exposed thighs riveted me but I knew I had to leave. I did all I could just to dress and open the door.

As soon as I was down the stairs I wanted to go back and lie beside her but I forced myself to leave. I wasn't sure if it was my pride or anger that was driving me, but either way I felt rejected, and it hurt me deeply.

Once outside I saw the burnt metal remains of the car that was in flames the night before. I walked over to it and stopped. It was a carcass in the urban jungle stripped of everything of any value.

I turned to Christine's window hoping to see her standing there waving to me to come back but she wasn't and I didn't see her again for a long time.

# 13

## 1978
## Twenty-Five Years Old

IN THE END leaving behind his Park Avenue address and Manhattan was too much for Doctor Ianucci. Already packed and with a sister waiting for him in Pennsylvania he died in the hallway of his apartment slain by a massive heart attack the day he was to leave.

The doorman had come up to his apartment to help him with his luggage. The cab was waiting at the curb to take him to the airport.

The doorman pushed open the door finding Dr. Ianucci's motionless body crumpled on the well-polished wooden floor beside his suitcases.

I found out about his death through a letter sent to me by another student of his who I only briefly met at one of the doctor's salons.

He wrote of the details and shared with me in a phone call that summer on how the doctor saved him from despair by making him feel that his life was worthwhile despite his drug addiction. The former student also shared with me what the doctor truly thought of me. I was glad to learn that he felt I was a true poet and that was all that mattered to him.

Not long after I received a letter from the doctor's sister asking if my letters to him and my poetry could be put in his archives she created at a university near Pittsburg. I told her it was fine with me. She did send me a letter he wrote me that she found that he had never mailed.

The letter was all about my aunt's death and how he believed I should turn my back on it and never think about it again.

In the letter he wrote that he feared that if I learned why my aunt was killed it would be too late to do anything about it and I risked the chance that the truth would be too much for me and it was probably something better left alone.

He ended the letter making me promise him that I would no longer discuss or think about my aunt's death but to see my childhood as a loving and peaceful one and that despite my curiosity and quest for knowledge sometimes personal awareness can do more harm than good. He ended the letter by writing "Ignorance *is* bliss."

I dedicated my first novel to him. After it was published many years after his death I got a call from someone else that knew him well and wanted to thank me for the dedication.

He spoke about the doctor in flattering terms and reminded me what I meant to him.

I never took down his name or kept in touch. My memory of our interaction is only what the mind creates of an oral conversation. Not the sound of the voice at all though something of the tone of the conversation exists. More than anything I have an imagined image of a man on a phone sitting in some small room speaking to me.

Memory is like that. Parts made from what is made-up and some parts so real you can place yourself in the scene as if looking through a window and all you have to do is open it and introduce yourself to those on the other side.

Socrates said that, "The unexamined life is not worth living."

Of course some say, sure it is. Just live it.

# 14

## 2014
## Sixty-One Years Old

JUST LAST YEAR, I got a call from a Detective Jessica Morales asking if she could see me. She said that she had inherited my aunt's murder in the Cold Case Squad, taking it over from Detective Lambisi.

Instead of meeting at the precinct she suggested we meet at the Blue Bay Dinner on the Long Island Expressway Service Road.

I got there first and found a booth in the far corner. I was now in my early sixties and had lost thirty pounds since having been diagnosed with type 2 diabetes. I put myself on a stiff regiment of walking intensely every day for forty minutes, focusing on my writing and teaching and eating better.

I was now sleeping without medication and felt healthier realizing the disease was actually something I could control. I was so good at taking control of it that I was no longer diabetic but considered pre-diabetic by my doctor.

I ordered eggs and toast staying away from my favorite diner food of milk shakes and deserts.

It was a cold night. When Detective Morales walked through the diner doors her face was red from the wind chill. I waved to her and she walked over to me. I figured it was her since she was alone and exactly on time.

When she reached my booth I saw that she had a pleasant face with dark brown hair and oval shaped brown eyes. She wasn't slender but she wasn't overweight either. She had hips but they were proportionate to her waist. She had a pleasant voice not exactly melodious but easy on the ears. I also thought that her face was pretty with aquiline features only slightly altered by age. She had a soft nose and round lips and a dusky complexion.

After our introductions she told me that Manny Lambisi was at the World Trade Center during the attack on September eleventh and broke a leg. He never truly recovered and retired right afterwards with a disability.

She inherited my aunt's case two years earlier but it took time for her to get to it with the mass exodus of veteran detectives who were retiring leaving the homicide squads around the city, depleted of not only man power but of experience as well. She told me that the Cold Case Squad was nearly short of detectives.

"I can't believe it's ten years since I spoke with him," I said to her referring to Manny.

"A little more than ten," Jessica told me ordering only coffee.

I felt comfortable with her immediately. I'm not sure if it was because she was a woman or because of her demeanor but she was more relaxed and less confrontational then Manny had been.

"I can't believe you're still interested in my aunt's case," I said to her sipping my coffee.

"Someone was killed. It's my job to find out who did it," she said pulling out the same exact file I saw ten years earlier. "It doesn't matter how long it takes."

"What happen if the killer is already dead?" I asked.

"The case is still open. That's all that matters," she answered. Listening to her speak I heard two things: one was an accent clearly something she acquired growing up in the Bronx and the other was her breathing. She was a smoker or was once and it took a toll on her lungs.

"It's that simple?" I said.

"Yes, it is," she answered.

She was wearing a dark blue blazer with a blue sweater underneath it, dark pants and dark ankle length boots. She had large hands and I wondered if that helped her hold her pistol which I figured was on her belt.

The thought about her pistol made me remember how I wondered where Walsh's revolver was when he interviewed me all those years earlier.

"Let me ask you," I said. "Have you met with anyone else besides me?"

"Not yet." She placed the file on the table and looked up at me. I watched her warm eyes cool. She was pretty but she was also determined. "Mister Tucci, as you know no one believes your story about the cake. What was the real reason you went down to her house every Tuesday?"

I figured her to be in her early forties. She wasn't wearing a wedding ring and I imagined her to be a sensual young woman not that long ago. What I couldn't imagine was why she wanted to be a cop and more than that, why in homicide?

"It's time to tell the truth, don't you think?" she said.

Before my meeting with her I was thinking the same thing. Was it time to tell the truth? Or did it matter anymore? My aunt's death had nothing to do with me. My parents were gone and everyone who had anything to do with her death were probably dead as well.

But then I thought about Doctor Ianucci's firm advice in the letter he wrote to me. He warned me not to pursue the truth. It would only hurt me in the end.

“I went there every Tuesday after school to pick up an envelope,” I blurted out. Yes, it was time to tell the truth despite Doctor’s Ianucci’s warning mostly because I wanted to know who killed my aunt and *why* they did it as much as this detective.

Nothing in the world would change once the killer was found. Wars would continue. Disease and accidents would continue to take their toll on humanity. However, in my small part of that world I wanted to know because I found her and for no other reason despite my mentor’s warning.

“A white envelope?” she asked her voice emphasizing her eagerness to know more.

She moved to her right. She wrote something on her pad. I could feel the energy go up a notch. She was thrilled to hear something new from me.

“This is new information,” she stated.

I didn’t respond.

“What was in the envelope?” she asked clearly trying to maintain a matter-of-fact attitude.

“I don’t know,” I answered.

“You never asked?”

“Never,” I answered.

Now she looked up at me. “Never?”

“Never.”

Now she leaned back. “Why did you keep this from us?”

“My parents told me not to saying anything.”

“Mr. Tucci you were a grown man when Manny interviewed you. Why didn’t you tell him?”

I took a breath. I wasn’t exactly clear why I hadn’t. “To protect them, I guess. Perhaps because I didn’t think it mattered. Maybe because I didn’t want my life defined by something I had no control over.”

I could see in her eyes that what I said made no sense to her. She was angry or maybe annoyed that all these years I kept a central fact, a truth from her and her colleagues.

She moved forward. "Who gave you this envelope?"

"My aunt."

"All the time?"

"Every time," I answered.

"And who did you give it to?" she asked.

"My parents. If they weren't home I'd put it on the dining room table and go to my room to do my homework."

She showed me a page of her file. "Detective Lambisi wrote in his notes that there was a woman seen leaving your aunt's house after you left. He also wrote that you told Detective Walsh that you felt someone was in the living room watching you."

I looked away from her at my water glass.

"Did Manny tell you that this woman fit the description of your mother?"

"You know he did," I answered.

She smirked. "And was your mother home when you got there?"

I never answered that question when I was asked before. Now, I wanted to. "I don't know if she was home or not. But I am sure that I didn't see her when I got home that afternoon. I placed the envelope on the table and went to my room. She called to me later to get ready for dinner."

"Did your mother act oddly at dinner?"

I shook my head. "Not that I remember."

She leaned in again. "Look, I'm not saying or thinking your mother had anything to do with your aunt's death," she told me. She pronounced *aunt* like I heard other people of either color or Spanish say it. I pronounced the word as you pronounced it if referring to a bug. She gave it a flair that I had heard my whole life from people who weren't from my world and it interested me for the moment.

She continued. "I'm not suggesting anything about your mother. In fact, when you look for a murderer you look for motivation. I have no idea what the motivation would be if she did stick that knife into your aunt. What I am interested in is solving this case and since you have withheld testimony all these years I am pissed off. I am really pissed off Mister Tucci."

I saw her displeasure but it mattered little to me.

"You have no idea what was in the envelope?"

"None."

"Was it bulky?"

"I could feel something in it. Not sure what it was. Money perhaps. Paper. I don't know," I answered.

She looked at me as if I was a problem she had to solve; a puzzle she was determined to figure out. I know I confused her with my cryptic retelling of the past. What she didn't realize was that I was also confused and now I wanted to unravel the secrets of my childhood.

"There was no way my mother did what you're inferring," I said.

"You know what I don't understand, Mike? I don't understand why in all this time you didn't seem compelled or even interested in knowing the truth." With that she closed the file and focused on her pad.

"Do you know someone named Theodore Affirmo?"

I struggled with the name. "Ted?"

"I guess he could be called Ted," she replied.

"Why do you ask?"

"So you know him?"

I shrugged. "A little. From back then. He always seemed to be around."

"When did you see him last?" she asked.

"I'm not sure. I think I saw him about twenty years ago. That was the last time," I answered. I looked up at her remembering. "Wait, I got a call from him around 9/11. Right after it. It was odd."

"What was?"

I watched her with her hand frozen on the pen and then pen frozen on the pad.

"He sounded strange. Like far away. His voice."

"What did he say?"

"Not much. He just asked how I was," I answered.

"He died a month after 9/11," Detective Morales said.

Now I was curious. "Why did you ask me about him? I don't ever think about Ted. I haven't thought about him in years, until just now when you brought him up."

"He paid for your aunt's funeral. He paid for the burial plot and the coffin," she answered. "I asked because I thought it was odd. So did Detectives Walsh and Lambisi since he wasn't a blood relative to anyone remotely involved in this case."

I told her how I always felt odd around Ted. I told her how I didn't know much about him and how I once heard my parents argue about him being around me which I thought was strange. It was funny how of all memories I still had roaming around my brain that one was neatly tucked away.

I imagined how neurons roam around in the cerebral cortex storing particular facts and discarding others. It was peculiar how some experiences were like filmed scenes. They played out in my mind like short films. Even though I am an actor in them, I'm holding the camera watching, observing and looking at myself as if an unobtrusive and an aloof god. However, in this particular memory I'm swept into the events and the reason I kept it secure in my brain.

I am sitting in the shadows on the stairs listening to my parents talk in the living room out of my view. The both of them discussing Ted being around me and how it bothered them and how my mother told my father that he should speak to my Aunt Josie to make a point to him that Ted shouldn't be around when I was there.

I remember how my father asked how I took it that he was there as if I'd be effected by his presence while all the time I had no idea who he was and why he always seemed to look at me in this peculiar way.

I wasn't sure how I blurted this all out to Jessica but I did and she feverishly wrote it all down on her pad until it looked like she'd press the pen down through the yellow paper so hard she'd put a hole in it.

When I was done talking she asked me about my Aunt Josie's husband Frank and the talk that my father was his partner and I told her what my father told me just like I told Manny and soon the entire story of my life was playing out like some kind of blurry image and the only reflection I was sure about, the only one that made any sense was my own; or so I hoped.

I talked with Jessica Morales until midnight. I saw her eyes closing as we did speak. I saw her resisting sleep. She lived in the Bronx and still had a half hour ride home and yet she persisted in asking me everything, sensing that after decades I was ready to reveal some big truth.

But there was no *big* truth. There was only the whodunit with its endless conjecture and for me the most troubling thing was that the yarn was about me. I was lost in the woods for so many years, purposely not wanting to know the truth and now it struck me right in my ribs just like the knife in my aunt's chest. The knife was my own unexplainable decision to not pursue the truth, to find out why she was dead and who killed her.

That night I slept with the lights on. My room filled with so many people who knew what I didn't know. They weren't able to tell me what had happened and if I had anything to do with it.

You see it was then that I realized her death had everything to do with me. Maybe I always knew that and was afraid to accept it. Doctor Ianucci warned me it was all about me but now I was older and the warning seemed harmless.

However time, with all its relentless energy, was forcing me to confront why I made that walk every Tuesday, what was in the envelope and what it all meant.

# 15

## 1966
## Thirteen Years Old

ONE DAMP WINTER MORNING I was waiting for the Q12 bus to take me to Monsignor McClancy High School in Jackson Heights. I was fourth on a line that stretched down to around twenty people. They all stood silently in the dim morning light waiting for the bus to come up Sixty-fifth Place to the bus stop.

It was seven forty five in the morning which was the time I always stood on the line for the bus during the week so I could catch two more buses on my way to school and get to my home room by nine o'clock in the morning.

This one particular morning a teenage boy older than me walked toward the line and stopped when he reached a boy around my age who was facing the sidewalk. The older teen had short cropped hair. I didn't notice what he was wearing but I'm sure that unlike me he wasn't wearing a Catholic School uniform.

Without warning he threw his fist into the boy's face. The boy took the punch and didn't react though I could hear a groan.

The majority of people that rode the bus, in those days and still today are women, elderly men and kids on their way to school. However, I was still surprised no one said anything to the older teen no matter how intimidated they were. Then again, without saying a word, the older teen again hit the boy flush in the face but this time turned and walked in the direction away from the bus stop.

The cherub in me looked away but when I tilted my head to get a better look down the sidewalk I could see that the older teen was too far away to see me. So I stepped forward and took a long look at the boy he had hit.

The boy was slightly taller than me but like me he was carrying his lunch. He was also oddly stoic. When the bus appeared and stopped to take on passengers the line moved and so did he. We all crowded onto the bus and soon I lost track of when he got off.

I had forgotten all about the incident until it happened again a few weeks later. It was on the same bus stop on a dreary winter day when another teen, the same general age as the first one, seemingly came from out of nowhere, found the boy on line and punched him.

This time the boy was closer to me. It was hard for me to see firsthand and up close as the boy getting hit just took the punch once again flush on his face without moaning in pain or saying a word in defiance other than a slight groan which was all the more memorable since it came from this gut.

I took notice of this second older teen since he was closer to me and I could see a flash of anger in his eyes as he hit the boy a second time, now on the side of the head knocking the boy back off his feet. The boy who got hit didn't fall but he was clearly rocked back by the fist that hit him in between his ear and mouth.

This time the older teen mumbled something then hit the boy hard in the head a third time, turned and walked away just like the first had.

"Why did he do that?" I asked a young boy around my age that I had seen on and off on the bus but never spoke to before.

"He deserves it," the young boy answered.

The young boy I had asked looked like a cherub like me though he had a harder look in his eyes than I imagine I had. He had a larger brow and very dark eyes and looked down when he spoke to me.

"What did he do to deserve getting hit like that?" I asked.

"Mine your own business," he answered.

"But I want to know," I said.

He still didn't look at me. The bus pulled up and we all started walking forward. "Sometimes people do things they can't get away with," he said shuffling his feet as he approached the steps. I followed closely behind him.

I was mystified by his answer and wondered if everyone on the bus knew something I didn't. I wondered if they knew about some dark, evil this boy had done and saw no reason to stop his punishment.

It was at that moment that I realized that he was getting hit as a penalty for something. I always wondered if he was being punished himself or perhaps he was taking the punishment for something his family had done.

I wanted to ask the boy himself so one morning on the bus I pushed my way through the crowd and found him. He was sitting quietly in the corner. No one had hit him that morning so he seemed at peace. I felt the bus sway and rock as he maneuvered through the narrow streets.

Though I wanted to ask him *why*? I couldn't. I wasn't that fully formed courageous person I was hoping to become someday so I just looked at him until I got off at my stop. As I did I glanced back at him. He seemed like anyone else, any young boy who was on his way to school.

I never saw him when I came home so I had no idea where he was traveling from other than my bus stop and I certainly didn't know where he was traveling to.

Months later, while hanging out down the park near my house, I asked another teen I had met briefly in the park that summer about the incident and asked if he had known about it.

"Everybody knows about it," he said.

"What did the kid do?" I asked.

"Something bad."

When I pushed him to define what something bad was he avoided answering. I figured it was because he didn't exactly know and perhaps had no idea.

"What happened to him?"

"His family moved."

I've never forgotten the event. If I close my eyes I still see it happening. Though the features of the boys who hit him as well as his own are nothing more sketches now I still think of who he was and why he was being punished.

# 16

## 1985
## Thirty-Two Years Old

CHRISTINE AND I BUMPED into one another on Fifth Avenue one late autumn night. She was well dressed in a long fur overcoat, dark dress and heels.

I was coming from a poetry reading I had just given in a small bar for a literary society and I had some people with me but I stopped them and rushed over to Christine as she was waiting on the corner for the light to change.

She gave me her phone number. I promised to call her that next week. The day I called we made plans to see one another that Saturday night.

I learned she has been married again and divorced again. From our conversation in a little Thai restaurant near her home in Brooklyn, I realized that she was becoming very aware of her physical beauty and how temporal it was in its very nature.

She was still stunning and I had to resist telling her as I looked across the table in the dim light while we shared a bottle of wine.

She invited me back to her apartment. It wasn't long before we were sitting on her sofa kissing and I realized how much I had missed her.

We made love with snow falling outside her window. After, we lay in one another's arms. We spoke about the past and how if we weren't exactly perfect for one another, we were at least *good* for one another.

I felt that, despite her narcissism, Christine had my well-being at heart and cared for me. That night I learned a few interesting things about her I never knew.

Christine's mother and father were deaf and dumb. Her father was a well chiseled award winning weight lifter from Sicily who came to this country and thrived. Her mother was as beautiful as Christine and the two stayed married for several years but then divorced not long after Christine was born.

I sometimes wondered if Christine was so sensitive because of the parents she had. When she spoke about her father that night I could see how vulnerable she was. She adored him but admitted it was difficult communicating with me. She signed when we met but I suspect that her deeper feelings might now have been easy to convey without expressing it vocally.

We saw one another a few more times and most of our conversation was about how she was surprised and delighted that young men were always trying to pick her up.

This vanity of hers was one way of holding to the thing she believed she was valued for; her physical allure. Her vanity didn't bother me since I could lie beside her and stare, but I was disappointed that she seemed only to define herself by accessing her own prettiness. If she had a tragic flaw that was it.

She never developed any skills or talents. Perhaps that was why she was attracted to me. My talent filled the gap in her soul.

I thought of my mother like that. She had no talents and, though neither did my father, my mother was such a confident person I suspected that she had a secret talent somewhere. A talent she protected and kept hidden from all those around her especially those close to her like her husband and her son.

Looking back, I never had a serious conversation about life with my mother. I never talked to her about love or death or even the mysteries of whom she was or who I was.

Our conversations were made up of sentences, complete and direct, but never philosophical or reflective.

Once I asked her about the white envelope. She was very ill with lung cancer and I needed to know. I had taken her to receive her radiation treatment and while we were waiting for the nurse I asked.

I was in my fifties when she was dying and when I asked she turned to me and simply said, "We all have white envelopes in our lives. Things tucked in secret that go away and come back like a song we remember, or a face. I see your father's face sometimes when I sleep now. I never saw it before. I'm dying. That's probably why I see it now."

My mother died very early one October morning. Three days before, I visited her. It was late in the afternoon and I could see that she was drained and disoriented. "Please leave me alone," she told me.

"Mom, you can't be by yourself. I'm staying until you don't need me. Or I can get a nurse to stay here with you."

"I don't want anyone in this house now. Leave me alone," she stated though her eyes were closed.

I managed to get a nurse through her insurance company and we set up a bed for my mother in the living room. The same one she watched TV in with my father, the same one I knew her to be so comfortable in.

My father died in the hospital my mother was to die in her house.

Just two days later the nurse called. I was there by seven and found my mother breathing heavily through her mouth. She was immobile and her breathing was hoarse and rough.

Her body heaved, making me realize that was the way we all died. Life left us. It left each organ, each cell slowly and methodically until there was nothing left but flesh and bone.

I called the local rectory, Saint Stanislaus Church, and luckily a priest answered. I asked him to give my mother last rites. The rectory was only a fifteen-minute walk away and the priest arrived just in time.

I thought my mother was unconscious when he reached her yet when he waved his hand over her in a sign of blessing, I saw her eyes open and widen and then her entire body lurched forward towards his palm.

"She knows I'm here," the priest said. He was from India, a man with warm dark eyes, a thin frame and a glorious hopeful smile.

I wanted to take my mother's hand and grasp it but there was nothing in my brain. Nothing. I repeated silently Rossetti's lines of poetry. "From perfect grief there need not be / Wisdom or even memory."

I watched as she heaved gently one last time and all life left her body. The second preceding that event my mother was no longer my mother. Her body no longer belonged to the woman I knew all my life.

I walked the priest out to the sidewalk and thanked him. He walked back to the rectory. Alone, I stood in the early morning sunlight listening to the sound of birds blasting their songs in the trees. I could think of nothing else but my mother's death.

I felt a grief and a loss that hallowed out the early morning. The life I once knew was now over.

~ ~ ~

One afternoon Christine called to tell me that she had heard from Ted. When she told Ted she had seen me he had invited us for drinks that coming Friday. I had no overwhelming need to see Ted but Christine persisted, telling me that he had helped her find her current job so she felt he was entitled to some of her time.

When I told her to go alone she made it clear that the reason he was inviting us for drinks was specifically to bring me along. Curious what that meant, I agreed to go.

We met Ted at a penthouse night club off of First Avenue in Manhattan on Thirty-fifth Street. It was on the twenty-ninth floor in a residential building that rose up alongside the East River. It was a narrow, solid looking structure with a light brick façade. The lobby was art deco.

The room itself was dimly lit, affording an expansive view of the Upper East Side. The tail lights of cars running uptown dominated the view along with the yellowish lit windows of the tall apartment buildings to either side of the avenue. The river itself was a dark, murky presence stretching across the night. Queens was on the other side of the river and its lights intermittently broke the darkness.

Both Christine and I were surprised that Ted was not alone. He had a woman with him. I had never seen her before. She was slight with light brown hair clearly dyed to hide the natural gray a woman her age would acquire.

Once we were seated at the table she couldn't take her eyes off of me. She hardly noticed Ted and occasionally she gave Christine a generous smile but all of her attention was on me.

It didn't dawn on me at first, but soon I realized that the reason for our get-together was for her to meet me so as the night moved on I gave her more of my attention.

She was petite and pretty. She had what everyone calls a heart shaped face. Her smile was oddly demure and her voice had the roughness of a smoker, though she didn't have a cigarette the entire evening.

She hardly spoke about herself and spent most of the evening asking me about my poetry and what I was doing with my teaching and in general what I was doing with my life.

Ted ordered drinks for us all and seemed pleased with himself for some reason. He also was unusually quiet. I had always remembered him being outgoing and fond of attention. But this night, with this new woman at his side, he was more reserved than ever before.

Her name was Helen and I didn't learn much more about her that entire evening other than she was born and raised in Brooklyn.

There was a piano player in the far corner of the room and couples were dancing.

Christine asked me to dance. Once on the floor she confided to me that though Helen was personable and very nice she had an odd feeling about her and she couldn't explain it. She asked me if I had the same reaction.

"She won't take her eyes off of me. Her look is warm though. Very warm. Nothing scary," I said.

"Same here. It's as if she really wants to know who I am. Such an odd thing coming from a stranger," Christine said.

Back at the table Christine turned to Ted and Helen. "How do you two know one another?" she asked.

"We met back in high school," Helen answered.

"But you never mentioned her, Ted," Christine said.

"We lost touch over the years," Helen said in a sharp tone making it clear to me she wanted to talk about other things.

I watched Ted as Helen spoke. His eyes drifted away, an odd sadness flew across them as if he was struck by a memory that haunted him and it had to do with Helen.

After I returned to the table, Helen asked me to dance. I wasn't surprised. Once on the dance floor she held tightly my left hand, her right hand firmly across my waist.

We danced in silence for a few moments until she looked up into my face. She was lighter than I thought she'd be. She was gliding as if giddy and I had to look down at her when we spoke.

"Your hair is so long," she smiled. "They let you wear it like that where you teach?"

"In the college? Sure. It's not that long, is it?" I smiled.

She shook her head. "I'm glad you are happy with your life. You seem so. And you're poet! How exciting," she exclaimed sincerely pleased.

"How long do you know Christine?" she asked.

"It's been years now."

"Are you a couple?"

I smiled. "It's been on and off."

"She is certainly beautiful."

"She is."

"Are you happy, Michael?"

I was so touched by her sincerity I could only nod that I was.

When we left we took the elevator down to the lobby and even inside the elevator I felt Helen's eyes on me, a perpetual smile on her face.

Down in the lobby we said our *goodnights* and Helen took hold of my hand and squeezed it without saying a word.

Walking to my car I felt her eyes on my back so I turned. I can still see her standing on the corner with Ted waiting to cross. Ted's eyes were focused on the other side of the street while Helen's were on me.

I could see her standing under the street light, amber rays falling across her face, the blast of car lights drenching her. She seemed to be looking past me, perhaps into the past or even the future, whatever she saw I was ignorant of it.

# 17

**2014**
**Sixty-One Years Old**

DETECTIVE JESSICA MORALES called me a few weeks after we had met the first time. This time we agreed to meet in Bowne Park in Bayside. The park was located in the middle of residential streets that had the feel of privacy and middle class aloofness. Elm trees were scattered around the well-kept ground and an actual pond filled with turtles and geese was in the center. It was an unusually balmy day for January so we sat on a park bench sometime around eleven o'clock in the morning.

I called her mostly Jessica with the occasional *detective* thrown in when I felt the need to be formal. She was wearing the same dark blue skirt and boots from when I met her the first time but this time she was wearing a beige sweater instead of a sports jacket. There were circles under her eyes probably from long hours and lack of sleep. However, her soft nose and gentle eyes made her luminous. Oddly, I was attracted to her despite our age difference. When she wasn't putting up the defensive poster of a cop, she was actually very warm and gentle.

In the daylight I could see a sparkle in her eyes that radiated curiosity along with intelligence, but also there was a darker gleam to her look I hadn't noticed the first time we met.

I wasn't sure where it came from and then figured it was probably put there by all of her dealings with the abysmal behavior of criminals and the damage they did to their victims, or perhaps something inside her own nature that made her pursue a career where she continually had to deal with the ugly side of human nature.

I sat back and watched her eat an Italian hero sandwich. She told me she picked it up at the Italian deli a short walk away. "Ted, *our* Ted, was married, did you know that, Mike?" she asked sipping a diet Coke.

"I had no idea," I told her.

"He was married from 1950 to 1970."

"Okay."

She continued to eat. "His wife was named Helen. I saw their marriage license."

I recalled the woman Helen I met that night Christine and I met Ted and her. I had no idea they were married. In fact, I had met Helen years after she and Ted were divorced if those dates were correct.

"Did you ever meet her?" Jessica asked.

I nodded. I told her about the night we went dancing. "That was after they were divorced. Years later, actually."

"Interesting," was all she said.

I shrugged my shoulders. "What does this have to do with anything?"

Jessica nodded. She was chewing as she did. Her eyes got bigger. She focused on a notepad she placed on her lap. "This Helen knew your Aunt Josie."

Jessica turned her gaze on me. The sun was behind the top of the elm. "She would fit the description of the woman seen leaving the house the afternoon your aunt was killed."

I absorbed what she said but I was perplexed by what she was suggesting. "Isn't that a stretch? Also, why would she kill my aunt?"

"I'm looking into that now," Jessica answered. "One thing I do know is that Helen Carlson is alive. She lives in an extended care facility at North Shore University Hospital."

I made a face. "Why didn't Manny know this?"

"He did. I found this in his notes. But he never had the chance to follow up on it with 9/11 and his disability. He made a lot of notes and I'm slowly getting to them all."

She placed her nearly eaten sandwich down on her lap. "I think we should go see her."

"*We* should go see her?"

Jessica nodded. "Yes. Now that you tell me that Ted introduced you to her. The fact that he had made a point of you meeting her and what you told me about how she acted towards you, I think it worth a shot to talk to her."

I got her point. "She might know something."

"Exactly," Jessica stated.

"When are we doing this?" I asked.

"You check your schedule and I'll check mine. They must have visiting times."

I nodded. "And let's have lunch before. Or dinner afterwards."

Jessica frowned. "Why?"

"I want to get to know you better," I told her.

"Why?"

"You just said that," I replied.

"I know. *Why*, Mike?"

"Because I want to get to know you."

For the first time since I met her I saw Jessica go still.

"I find you attractive. Very, actually."

She still didn't say anything.

"I know I'm older than you but in a way that's a good thing," I smiled.

"For you it's a good thing. You get a nice sexy body," she smiled back.

I chucked. “So I have a chance to see it?” I asked.

“Don’t count on it,” she answered with a grin.

We didn’t say much the rest of the time we spent in the park. I imagined that we had already said more than enough. I figured I surprised her with my interest in her and she shocked me that it seemed somewhat mutual.

We made an appointment a few days later to go see Helen Carlson in Extended Care at North Shore University Hospital. On the afternoon we were supposed to go Jessica called me to cancel. Her son had a fever and she was running to a doctor’s appointment.

She suggested I go alone since she had already made an appointment and, despite my reluctance, I decided to make the trip.

From my apartment it wasn’t too long a ride to the hospital and once I parked I walked up the hill to the Extended Care building which was at the far end of the quiet hospital grounds.

The sky was overcast with the threat of snow so I made my way quickly to the entrance and was greeted by a receptionist at front desk. She was a slight Indian woman in her twenties.

I explained who I was and lied telling them that Jessica, Detective Morales, was running late. The receptionist wasn’t fazed at all and directed me to a room. I slowly found my way there.

I argued with myself that the entire notion of the trip was ridiculous and at the very least pointless but my life had slowed down a lot and I had the time to pursue just about any lead that might shed some light on my aunt’s death.

I found the room and stopped outside. Like most people hospitals made me uncomfortable. The atmosphere of death and dying and more than that the sense of hopelessness chilled me.

However, I stood in the open door and saw that the bed closest to the door was empty so I walked deeper into the room and saw a wash of light coming in from the closed window.

The light distracted me and I didn't see Helen at first but there she was, sitting in a chair looking out the window. She turned to me. Though she had aged and was probably in her eighties with wrinkles and nearly white hair I recognized her immediately.

She was in a white and blue robe and slippers. She turned to me when I entered the room and smiled but she didn't say anything.

"Excuse me," someone said behind me. I turned to find a nurse bringing a tray into the room. She was a black woman, overweight but moving quickly enough, as she walked passed me to Helen. "Are you a relative?" she asked as she set the tray down in front of Helen, the tone of her voice filled with a clear sense of authority.

"Oh, no," I replied.

"Then what are you doing here?" she asked.

"I knew Helen from a long time ago. I was here to ask her a few questions," I responded. "It's a police matter. Detective Morales is running late."

"You don't know then," the nurse said turning Helen to her left so she could face the tray.

"I don't know what?" I asked.

"Helen has Alzheimer's," the nurse told me.

"Oh," I muttered. I shot her a slight smile and left the room. But before I did I glanced at Helen. Though I just learned she probably had no idea, I couldn't shake the feeling that she did know me. Her smile was infectious and it made me leave the room carrying it with me.

I called Jessica that night. Her son was feeling much better but still had to stay home from school. I told her what had happened. I could hear her disappointment but then she said, “The woman knows something even though she might not remember it.”

“Why do you say that?” I asked.

Jessica was quiet and then said, “It’s a hunch I have.”

“But if she can’t tell us anything what do we do?”

Jessica told me that even if Helen might not be able to tell us anything, her *life* might. She explained that she needed time to look into her life and see what she could find about her and her relationship with my Aunt Josie, Ted and perhaps my parents.

I wasn’t sure why Jessica mentioned my parents but she did and it made me uneasy. Once again these cops kept pointing a finger in the direction of my mother and father and it irritated me.

Jessica and I ended the conversation with a plan to meet over the weekend when her son was going to spend time with her ex-husband.

I hung up and sat down in the dark. I allowed the silence to swallow me. I wanted to give myself the complete presence of mind to seek images from my past that might help explain lost truths.

I hadn’t realized that being in that room alone with Helen that afternoon unnerved me. I wasn’t sure if it— as if I was flashing forward to the loneliness waiting for me in my old age, or that she was some sort of representative of an enigma; so obvious and yet so elusive.

I thought of writing poetry so I put on the lamp on my desk and sat down. I knew that all inspiration came from some feelings that was always there under the surface and all it needed to be released was some gentle nudge, usually an emotion.

Helen was my muse that evening. I allowed my subconscious to take over thinking of what it might be like if

I were sitting in that chair at the window looking out to the fading sunlight without friends or family around me.

Did her disease save her from loneliness or did the disease bring about a more profound aloneness? This was the topic of my poem. I started a poem by searching for an image and I found one. It was Helen. In the poem she was an immobile smiling woman locked in what was neither the present or the past and certainly not the future.

She felt everything and nothing at the same time. She was neither a child nor an aged senior but something so profoundly in the moment that that elusive element called memory didn't mean anything and yet it meant everything.

When I was done writing the first draft of the poem I forced myself to get up from the chair. I hadn't moved for nearly an hour.

I looked out the window, it was already dark. I wasn't hungry and I wasn't thirsty. I thought of Helen, realizing it was only the second time I had seen her in my life and yet now she might hold the key to my aunt's death.

It made me wonder why this woman who I knew nothing about was so important to me. I wondered what she could mean to me both practically and metaphysically.

I was unable to relax and quickly went back to my desk and confronted the poem. There was so much more to mine from my subconscious. So I did just that, digging deeply into the realm of both the imagined and the imaginable hoping to find something that made sense because that night I felt that nothing had.

I don't know what time it was but when I turned to the window it was snowing. The balmy day turned into a snowy night and the silence and the snow brought me back to a similar night many years earlier when I was lying naked beside Christine looking out her window at the falling snow.

# 18

## 1985

## Thirty-Two Years Old

“WILL WE REMEMBER THIS MOMENT?” Christine asked me. Our bodies were entwined and our lips were just seconds earlier locked together.

I felt the heaving rush of wanting to kiss and suck every part of her body. Her nipples, the whole of her breasts, her thighs, her vagina, her ass, the nape of her neck, her toes and where ever I could place my mouth.

I felt that way about Christine. What I felt for her was a lust that I was always looking to indulge myself in. Though only a year or so older than me I felt her to be the perfectly formed woman in every way. I felt it the moment I saw her in my Aunt Josie’s backyard that night a thousand moons ago.

And now she was nude and underneath me and I placed my penis in her even though I felt awkward and nearly embarrassed by my lust.

When I told her that time I wanted to marry her she said to me, “You’ll stop getting turned on by me. It happens that way to men. You’ll look for other women.”

“How can anyone take your place?” I asked.

“It happened to my husband and he told me every day how much he wanted me,” she said, talking about James, the man she married after Louis Jr.

Christine had married a mobster's son. The son, Salvatore, though handsome and charming, was a drug addict, something Christine swore she didn't see until they were married. He made his living running numbers for his father. After only four months of being married he told her he was going out for a pack of cigarettes and never returned.

Six months later Salvatore called Christine and despite his father demanding that he return to his marriage he never did. Less than a month after his call to Christine he was killed on the Long Island Expressway in a car accident. The driver who hit him was drunk and survived with only bruises.

That driver in the accident was black and Salvatore's father was enraged that he had killed his son. One summer night walking from his home to a local bodega he disappeared and was never heard from again and his body was never found.

Salvatore's father was enamored with Christine and to get her through her hard times he gave her money. When he hosted big stakes poker games in his social club he paid her to bring food and drinks to the players. Most of them were high rollers and healthy tippers. Some nights she'd walk out of a game with a thousand dollars in cash.

I thrust my hips forward with abandon wanting her to know that I had no control over my lust for her. I felt her hand on my ass as she gripped her fingers into my cheeks. When she did I lost control and gave myself over to her and came.

I breathed deeply and I soon went limp, feeling the sticky wetness from my seamen dripping onto my thigh and sliding off onto the bed.

"You came too fast," she said sharply. "I wasn't ready," she said.

I pushed off of her. My body was muscular from the last time I was in bed with her. I was in my thirties and spend my time in the gym creating the upper body I lacked when in my twenties. I grew a beard and kept it trim. My dark hair was still long and wavy. "I couldn't help myself."

"You are old enough to know better. I'm here too, you know," she said.

I lie on my back and saw her face right up against mine. "Let's try again," she grinned, as her violet eyes bulging with deviousness.

She moved her head down my body and put her mouth around my penis. She shifted her hips over me so that her belly was on my belly and her inner thighs spread across my face.

I could smell my own seamen but it didn't matter because I could also smell the aroma of her vagina and it made me eager again. I licked her vagina and placed my hands on her hips and pictured her derriere angled up in the air and the picture of her in that position drove me wild.

As she sucked on my penis I licked her and we created a rhythm driven by a lack of shame punctuated by a need to display to one another our shared openness.

I made her have an orgasm delighting in her moans of pleasure. She made me ejaculate again and I called out "Christ!"

"He had nothing to do with it," she murmured.

Later that night, trying to sleep I got up and found Christine's desk and while she slept I wrote a poem about her.

The next day I left it for her and she brought it up when we went to a café for morning coffee. Our feet made crunching noises under our boots as we walked through the several inches of snow.

"I'm your muse?" she asked.

"Yes," I told her.

Once in the café sipping our coffee again she told me that I was too sensitive for a woman like her. She had told me this once before, or so I remembered. She said that she needed a man to take care of her and a poet isn't the kind of man who could take care of any woman.

I was mortified and hurt. I was suddenly the sensitive cherub I once was all those years earlier. Yet I knew there was a lot of truth to what she said. I was not the kind of man who would take care of a woman. I was a poet who, according to Baudelaire, should sit on a hill, study the clouds, and develop their sensibilities.

It was sometime during that period that Ted called Christine and invited us out and that was the night I saw Helen for the first time.

A few weeks after that night Christine and I drove to the beach. It was an odd thing to do in the middle of winter but the temperature shot up to fifty and the air was heavy and damp.

We parked the car and walked on the sand at Long Beach and sat down on the sand wearing our jackets, looking up at the night sky listening to the waves slowly come in.

Christine leaned back against me and looked straight out. I adored her profile and how her black hair fell across it dipping up and over her ear on one side. I nibbled her ear and placed my face right up against hers.

"I can't get that woman Helen out of my mind," she said.

"Why not?" I asked.

"It was the way she looked at me. I know you thought she looked at you in the same way but she couldn't take her eyes off of me. I think I know why now," she said. "I think she saw me as someone you loved."

I was confused. "Not sure what you mean."

"You never met her before, right?"

"Right."

"So why do I get the feeling that she knows you?"

I had no idea what to say or how to respond. "I don't know her, Christine."

"I know you don't. But she knows you. I am sure of it. So I asked Ted," Christine said turning her face to me.

"And what did he say?"

"It's what he *didn't* say that got my attention."

"Meaning?"

"He said he didn't want to talk about it."

We both grew quiet and allowed the gentle sounds of swaying surf fill the night air.

"I noticed how quiet he was around her that night," I said.

"And he made the point he wanted to see you or that *she* wanted to see you," Christine said.

That was about as far as we got that night talking about Helen. It is odd how years pass and people follow different roads and take different highways with their lives and never see one another even though they only live minutes or miles from one another.

I can't remember how Christine and I drifted apart back then, but we did. How each of us going our separate ways with separate people, each of us passing through life with our backs to the past but ironically heading straight for it.

~ ~ ~

The last time I saw her was when I was fifty years old. I was in a restaurant with a friend in Williamsburg, Brooklyn. We were just ordering when I heard a voice coming to me. I would recognize it anywhere. It was Christine's.

I turned around and scanned the dimly lit restaurant but I couldn't see her. So I changed seats with my friend telling him the entire story. I described her as beautiful and he was intrigued.

This time I looked in the direction of the voice. I narrowed my focus on a table of four where two middle-aged couples were sitting. One woman was plump and blond. So I looked closely at the other.

I didn't recognize her at all but I did know her voice. It *was* Christine's. I tilted my head to look beyond my friend and there she was. However, she had changed drastically. Her sleek dark hair was now cut short. Her aquiline features were puffy and her face was no longer one that would launch a thousand ships.

I was stunned and yet at the same time relieved that the romantic pangs I had kept hidden for years for her were now lessened and in an instant relieved.

I tried to listen in on the conversation and it was clear that the man with her, ordinary but in shape was her husband. Christine herself was talking about illness and recovery.

Her voice, to me once melodic and intriguing though on the verge of being superficial, was now shoved aside by a rough-edge and sketchy sound; the kind that once you hear you never forget. She has also gained considerable weight and though dressed in black it couldn't hide her shape.

I explained it all to my friend, a fellow professor from the college, and he was sympathetic and understanding. Especially when I told him that I would like to leave the restaurant and find another.

When I got home that night I pondered the value of all those years I harbored feelings for her. I tried to put a value on her beauty and my obsession. I struggled to understand romantic love and what it meant knowing that decades earlier my feelings for her meant the world to me.

I felt foolish and artificial telling myself I was a poet and I allowed these moments of shallowness. I tried to write a poem about my feelings about Christine and realized that my muse had become a nightmare worn down by time and mortality.

I was dumbfounded by my own ignorance. How silly I was that a woman's beauty captivated me when life was supposed to be about so much more. I wanted to punish myself for my longing but then a moment flashed when I realized that I should saver those times I had with her. Not only the romantic and sensual ones we shared but also how she thrust me back into my memories of all those years earlier, forcing me to confront the white envelope and what it all meant.

~ ~ ~

Three years later I got a call from Louis Jr. "She died yesterday morning. She's being laid out today and tonight at DeMarco's Funeral Home on Lorimer Street," was all he said to me.

I knew who he was talking about. "I'll be there."

When I entered the room I was surprised to see that the coffin was closed. The once beautiful Christine could no longer have her face seen by the world. Of course I was imagining all the awful reasons they may have had the coffin closed but I soon learned from Louis Jr. why it was.

He had lost considerable weight. He said that he was healthy and had lost it from a new diet regime. Sadness enveloped him. I could see that he had been crying.

The room was only sparsely filled. The dim lamp light from the tables created an almost Victorian atmosphere. A quick glance showed that the décor was mundane and placid. The room was a sad place for friends and family to say goodbye.

"She had only one request. She wanted her coffin closed," Louis Jr. told me.

He went on to tell me that she had a brain tumor and after the diagnosis her death was quick. "I still loved her you know."

I learned that night that Louis Jr. paid for all of Christine's hospital expenses and her funeral despite his remarrying.

I knelt down at the coffin. Louis Jr. placed a dozen photographs of Christine around the coffin and on the table beside it. He wanted the world to see what she looked like before age and death took away her looks and her life.

I decided not to go to the funeral mass and not to attend the burial the next morning. I couldn't accept any more how life took away people from me, changed them all the while leaving me alone only with my memories.

# 19

## 2014
## Sixty-One Years Old

JESSICA ASKED ME TO MEET HER at a storage facility in South Brooklyn where the Brooklyn Navy Yard used to be. When I got there she was already inside a small storage room that was only partially filled with several boxes.

"What are we doing here?" I asked.

Jessica explained that she found a notation in Manny Lambisi's notes that he had located a ticket to a storage unit buried in a file Walsh had managed to uncover before the case hit a dead end for him.

It took her some time but one of the officers who worked in the file department came across the storage unit ticket and gave it to Jessica. Jessica then tracked the ticket to this particular unit and found that the room belonged to and was paid for by Ted.

She learned that he had been paying for the unit even after he died putting money aside for it to pay it automatically from an account he had set up. Jessica was of course curious so she went to the unit and called me when she discovered something interesting. The account was in Helen's name.

"It's paid for up until she dies," Jessica told me.

"She wouldn't recognize any of this stuff even if she was here," I said looking around the very small room.

It contained only several brown cartons filled with papers, some cheap jewelry and photographs.

Jessica had already moved some cartons around. "Let see what we can see."

She pushed through the files and papers focusing on the photographs. Most of them were aging so badly they were faded and yellow.

One photo album did look in good enough shape to peruse through and Jessica opened it. She put it down on the floor, dusted it off and despite the unit being cold we both sat on the floor next to one another on either side of the album.

I reacted when Jessica turned to a page of a bride posing with her bridesmaids. "Do you recognize this woman?" she asked me pointing to the bride.

I looked closer in the bright yellow light. "It could be my aunt," I told her. I could see the round chubby face, the thick eyebrows, and the bulky body. "Yes, that *is* her."

"I was hoping it was her," Jessica said.

I looked even closer. "And that's my mother," I said pointing to a woman beside my aunt.

"The bridesmaid," Jessica said.

It was my mother alright. Smiling with her bright eyes and her heart shaped face. She was young and beautiful back then.

I scanned the photograph. There were several other women with brown hair and oval faces. Only one was blond looking like a visiting foreigner to this Italian American wedding.

Jessica pulled the plastic off the photograph and slipped it out of the album. She turned it around. There was handwriting on the other side of it. It was legible enough to read.

Names were printed on the back. I saw my mother's name next with several next to the word *bridesmaids*. Then I read *maid of honor* and *Helen* written next to it.

Jessica read it just as I did. She looked at me. "The *maid of honor* isn't your mother. It's Helen."

I took the photograph from her and turned it around. I scanned the bridesmaids and this time I did recognize my mother. She was on the far left. So I looked closer at the woman I thought was my mother. They were nearly identical at first glance but in looking closer I could see that Helen had a thinner face and though they were both smiling and their smiles were identical as well, Helen had more angular features.

Also my mother had freckles which I didn't know she had back then or perhaps as the cherub I just never noticed.

"Your mother and your aunt and Helen knew one another as young women. Not only knew one another but were also pretty close friends. Or so it seems from this wedding photograph," Jessica said.

She paged through it again and we took our time over each photo. Josie was in most of them and so was her new husband Frank. In one photograph I recognized my father dancing with my mother.

"Helen caught the bouquet," Jessica asked.

She was pointing to a photograph on the page alongside it where Helen was reaching up to catch the bouquet. She had caught it.

"Is this Ted?" she asked. She pointed to the next photograph where a man was hugging Helen as she held the bouquet.

I looked closer. "Yes, that's him."

Jessica took her own close look then turned the pages until she came to the last one. In it, my aunt, Helen and my mother stood arm in arm facing the camera.

Dressed in white my aunt beamed with joy. All the women beamed with joy.

We both found it interesting that these three posed together and alone without the rest of the bridesmaids or the men.

Jessica struggled to get to her feet. I managed to move quickly and stood up beside her.

She placed the photo album in her backpack as I glanced around the room.

"What's going to happen to this stuff?" I asked.

"When Helen passes, and if there's no will making a claim on it, whoever owns this place will auction the stuff off. Or destroy it," Jessica answered. "I want to go through all of it before that happens."

When we closed the door and Jessica locked it I followed her outside. "I wonder why Ted kept this for her," I asked.

Jessica shook her head. "I hope we find out the answer to that question and hopefully that might help us find out who killed your aunt."

~ ~ ~

A couple of days later I got a call from Jessica to meet her. She said she wanted to meet me at the Blue Bay Diner right after sunset.

When I got there she was sitting with a file in a booth in the corner. As I walked up to her I could see a very serious look on her face. It unnerved me.

When I sat down she pushed a file across the table. "Open it," she said.

I opened the file. I looked closely unable to digest what I was seeing. "My birth certificate?"

"A copy," she said.

I saw photographs of a baby taken in a photo studio.

"I imagine that's you," she said.

I saw photographs of my baptism and confirmation. I assumed they were photographs of me.

Jessica handed me a small book. I took it. It was a hard copy volume of my poetry printed in limited edition.

"Why does she have a book of my poetry?" I asked.

I put it down and picked up the birth certificate.

"Why is stuff about me in Helen's storage unit?" I asked.

I looked up at Jessica. It was clear that she was struggling with what to say to me. She gestured to the birth certificate in my hand.

"Helen's your birth mother," she told me.

I read *Helen Carlson* under *mother* and *Theodore Affirmo* under *father*.

"You were adopted by your parents, Mike. It's all there. Read it closer. The date of birth, your weight and height, hair and eye color. Is it accurate?"

I was unable to move. "It can't be." I looked up at her. "Somebody made this up."

"I know this is hard but look it over for me, please."

I read it over. The dates were all accurate.

"You were born on Twenty-Third and Lexington Avenue March eighth in nineteen fifty-two at The Woman's Infirmary Hospital. Unfortunately the hospital doesn't exist anymore so it would be hard to find those records without a long search but that birth certificate looks real enough to me," Jessica told me.

The waitress came for my order but I couldn't even look at her. Jessica waved her off. "I'm sorry you had to learn all this in *this* way but now I need to find out why your aunt was murdered and if your adoption had anything to do with it."

"Helen is my mother?"

"So it seems."

I felt sweaty, uneasy, and dizzy. I looked around the diner as if it were some alien world I suddenly had to adjust to.

"I am now sure it was either your mother as you call her or Helen who was the woman seen leaving the house. I am sure one of them killed your aunt. If I can find a motivation I will know who it was. If I can find out what was in that envelope I will find the motivation."

"I don't want to know anymore," I told her.

"I now know why you never wanted to know. Maybe all the while somehow you knew it was all about you. I don't know. I just think that maybe that part makes sense to me now," Jessica said to me.

When the waitress came back I didn't order anything but water. I couldn't eat. I couldn't think either.

I could hardly hear Jessica explaining that she found a small note book. In it was a log. It had numbers written down each page and from what she could make of it they looked like payments.

According to Jessica who looked at an old calendar the notations in the log book coincided with the dates on those Tuesdays I went to my aunt's house to pick up the envelope.

Jessica figured that the amounts next to the dates were dollar amounts in cash that was put in the envelope.

"I'm thinking if I am right Helen was paying your mother to raise you. She paid for her to take care of you. But something went wrong. Perhaps Helen wanted you back. Perhaps your mother wanted to keep you. Yet even if one of those things are true it doesn't help us figure out why your aunt was killed," Jessica said.

"My aunt was the go-between," I said.

"Yes, the go-between among friends," Jessica answered.

"Ted was not my father. That man could not be my father. My father was my father. I don't know if any of this matters," I said to her.

Jessica nodded. "After all these years I can understand that. They're all dead now. There's no one to ask. There's no consequence."

"Yes, so who cares who killed my aunt?" I said getting heated up.

"You were the prize, Mike. These women fought over you and maybe even one of them murdered your aunt over you. And then when I find that out, it's over."

"Over for you. Not for me," I stated.

Jessica placed one last thing in front of me. It was a notebook.

"She wrote poetry," she told me. "Helen wrote poems."

I flashbacked to that time years ago when she and I had that dance together. I could still see the look of delight when she mentioned me writing poetry. It was an affirmation that I was her son because she loved poetry and wrote it too.

~ ~ ~

I couldn't sleep that night, kept awake by memories. They were all a lie and, knowing that, I was uneasy and afraid. My entire life had been a lie. Who I was, who my parents were and where I was truly from.

I read Helen's mawkish lyrics written in perfect penmanship learned in Catholic school back then. The poetry was obvious and amateurish. It was clear the poet, Helen, was not educated in the tradition of the great poets of the centuries but still she filled an entire notebook with her feelings written in free verse and some rhyming poems. The poems were about loss, giving away a *part of her* to the future.

Knowing her only from that one meeting I did see her in her poems. The feelings were heartfelt, the emotions unrestrained and the poems asked broad philosophical questions about the meaning of life and the tragedy of betrayal.

I always wondered why I was a poet since neither of my parents even enjoyed reading. In fact, that very fact made me protect my talent and hide it from them for as long as I could.

I thought now that perhaps my father tried writing because he knew Helen wrote poetry and he wanted to imitate her so one day he could say to me that it was clear that he was my *true* father?

Something else came to mind. One distinct memory rose out of my cerebral cortex and that was when I was very young I had read about a writing school on a matchbook cover I found in my mother's kitchen.

It was an ad for "learn to write home writing school." The ad stated that you could join the school and learn to write fiction and poetry simply by corresponding with a teacher through the mail.

I was probably only around fourteen or so and called the phone number on my own and set up an appointment with a salesman who would come to my house. Since I was a minor he had to meet with my father.

The salesman stopped by the house on a Saturday afternoon and he was slick. He had a round face, short hair combed back and I can still see his curious gaze fixed directly on me. He complimented my father on his house and I could see my father puff up at the suggestion that he was successful.

I sat silently hoping to get the approval of the gregarious smiling salesman and I was naïve enough to think that it mattered what he thought. He was just looking to sign me up and get a down payment for my first class.

Looking back I realize that day was the first that my father found out I wanted to write. He dealt with this odd announcement on my part very well suggesting to the well-dressed salesman in his suit and tie that he could certainly afford my signing up for the correspondence class.

I can't remember how much the course cost. I believe it would be paid in stages with me given a writing assignment and then I'd pay for the critique of my work by some professional I would never meet in person.

When the salesman left that day I was sure I was on my way to learning how to write. They shook hands and my father said it looked good and that he'd be in touch about my enrollment as soon as he talked it over with my mother.

That evening the three of us met in the living room and my father explained to my mother about my interest in the writing school.

She sat across from me stoned faced and said, "We can't afford it."

I was shattered.

"He's not a writer," she said.

"It can be a hobby," father told her.

"I'm not paying for a hobby."

"But I like writing poetry," I told her.

She glared at me. "You aren't and you will never be a poet," she stated as if she could create the truth by force of will.

That was all I remember from that afternoon. I never took the course, but I went on to be a published poet and never mentioned that afternoon to either of them ever again.

I wanted to write that night when I learned neither one of them were my blood parents but I couldn't. Instead I thought of a poem by Dante Gabriel Rossetti which went, "From perfect grief there need not be / Wisdom or even memory."

No one had died but I felt that I had. I grieved the demise of the person I thought I was. I didn't want to accept that Helen and Ted were my biological parents. I didn't know them. They seemed like nomads drifting through the veiled past without direction or significance.

Yet, before I slept, hoping that sleep would ease my new wounds, a thought crossed through my mind probably through exploding neurons. I wanted to know why they gave me up and allowed someone else to claim me as their own. I wanted to know what wrong I had committed that I was unworthy of their patience, their time and their love.

# 20

## 2014
## Sixty-One Years Old

JESSICA AND I MET AGAIN but only after a few days. I had called her a few times inviting her to dinner but she didn't call me back right away. It didn't take long for me to figure out that the notion of starting some kind of romantic interlude was not enticing to her. More than that, she had a young son to protect and that thought probably hurt me more than any other.

I was someone's young son and they didn't protect me. Or so it seemed to me the day I realized why she wasn't calling me back. Unless there was some other reason I didn't know. One afternoon she did call me to tell me she wanted me to meet her at the assistant district attorney's office in Kew Gardens later that week.

~ ~ ~

The office was near the Queens Criminal Court on Queens Boulevard. The district attorney was a young Asian woman dressed in a dark blue pants suit. I wondered if dark blue was the color all women had to wear who worked criminal justice.

Amy Wong was slim with short black hair and coal dark eyes. She wore glasses and was younger than Jessica.

Both ladies in a conference room behind a medium sized wooden table. After some quick introductions Amy Wong said, "You withheld information from this office for several decades, Mister Tucci, information that might have moved this case along a lot quicker. However, Detective Morales and I have decided that to bring charges against you would not only be unnecessary but pointless."

I turned to Jessica who was watching me the moment I entered the room. I decided to be aggressive and fight fire with fire. "Who killed my aunt, Ms. Wong?"

Jessica spoke up. "We're closing the case."

"After ruining my life you're closing the case?" I shot back.

"Mister Tucci, the woman we believe to have adopted you is dead. Yesterday we received medical records concerning your birthmother Helen Carlson and for all intent and purposes Alzheimer's has made prosecuting her a moot point," she stated.

"So you believe she killed my aunt?"

Ms. Wong nodded. "Yes."

"And why did you come to this conclusion? I believe I have the right to know."

Jessica spoke up. "You do." She glanced to Ms. Wong making it clear that though they had disagreed over it, I should know or not, she believed I had *every* right to know.

"We spent the last few weeks checking into public records as well as Helen Carlson's person effects," Jessica said. "Helen paid your mother to take care of you."

I nodded. "The white envelope."

"Yes," Jessica answered. "We believe she sent the money to Connie, your adopted mother, to take care of you."

"And they made me pick it up?" I grimaced.

"Perhaps only for convince sake," Jessica said.

"Ironic," I told her.

Jessica continued. "Perhaps one day she had plans to reclaim you. Either way, we believe that not long before her death your Aunt Josie tried to extort Helen for more money."

"Why?" I asked.

"Maybe she needed money and figured Helen and Ted were good for it."

"Did my mother know?" I asked.

"We don't believe Connie knew," Ms. Wong said.

"There's no evidence that she did, Mike," Jessica stated.

"You think that's why Helen killed my Aunt Josie?" I asked, clearly not believing it was enough of a reason for her to do something like that.

"No, Michael. It seems your aunt threatened Helen," Jessica said.

"Threatened her how?" I asked.

Jessica placed an old folded up yellowing letter on the table in front of me.

"We found a letter in the storage unit. It's the extortion note your aunt wrote Helen. Helen saved it. In it your aunt writes that if Helen doesn't pay her the extortion money she was going to tell you when you grew up that Helen was your mother and that she abandoned you because she didn't love you," Ms. Wang stated.

"That could put any woman over the edge," Jessica said. "I'm a mother, I know."

I sat back. It did make sense. Or some of it did.

"Why did Helen give me up?" I asked.

I saw that look on Jessica's face. She knew something and it was probably difficult to tell me but I had asked.

"Do you need to know?" she asked.

"Of course I do," I said. "We're not talking about some stranger. We're talking about me. I feel as if I am in surgery while awake and conscious. Yes, I *need* to know."

These women were taking my entire life apart, bit by bit, and it was damaging my soul. Not just the women in the room but the women in my life before I had a life. Connie, Helen, my Aunt Josie. I was the perennial pawn in their grips. They held and kept me in perpetual limbo and now I wanted answers.

"It's only conjecture now but Ted Affirmo was arrested for sodomy and statutory rape in nineteen forty-seven. Today it'd be better known as child molestation. However, there was no conviction and all charges were dropped," Ms. Wang stated. "Probably because the victim or the parents of the victim refused to testify."

"He was arrested again in nineteen fifty-five and again the alleged victim and probably their parents failed to appear in court and all charges were dropped," Jessica said.

"He moved out of state for several years. We're not sure if he was ever arrested or charged again," Ms. Wong told me.

Jessica read the look on my face. "What?"

I had a flash of a rainy afternoon. I saw a little boy with his school bag with sagging shoulders and sad eyes sitting in the front seat of a car looking up at a man. I was that little boy.

"Mike?" I heard Jessica say.

I looked at her.

"It's over," she told me. "It's been over a long time ago. You can forget everything now."

"Forget?" I said to no one but myself.

"You're free to go," Ms. Wang told me. "In a couple of days you'll receive a letter from this office stating that your testimony was well documented and the case concerning your aunt's homicide is officially closed and the person responsible for her death, Helen Carlson, is mentally unfit for prosecution."

I didn't move. Sunlight drenched the antiseptic room from its large windows yet it exuded no warmth at all. The brightness itself was evasive. I fought feelings of humiliation with my silence.

I didn't want to move yet I forced myself to stand. I had had enough. I walked to the door. I stopped. I turned. "When did Helen give me to my mother? I mean, to Connie and Ed?"

"On your second birthday," Jessica said.

"I'm sorry," Ms. Wang said.

This time I saw a flicker of emotion in her eyes. It mattered to her, it seemed.

"Take care, Mike," Jessica said to me. I saw in her eyes that I was a damaged man and in all likelihood not someone she wanted to know any deeper.

"I never needed to know any of this. I hope you both know that," I told them and left the room.

~ ~ ~

I can't remember how long after but I did go one last time to see Helen. It was near spring and warm enough for her to be allowed to sit outside.

Before I entered the facility, I saw her in a wheelchair under a tree in the yard along the side of the building so I made my way over.

A nurse had just left and she was sitting there looking away from me in the shade of a large oak. I walked quietly over to her not exactly sure why I was there but knowing that I-wanted to ask her something one last time.

When I turned she saw me. Her eyes were dulled over and all animation seemed to have fled her very being. She seemed complacent and nearly comatose but I still approached.

I found a chair and sat. We were face to face and for the first time in my life I knew who she was. She was my natural mother and I wanted to love her.

I wanted to tell her that I had grown up and moved away from the lie; though that was the biggest lie I could have told her. Yet, still, I wanted to comfort her and let her know it was all right and that I forgave her.

However, before I could say anything, I was possessed by panic. I had lied to myself. Nothing was alright. I was damaged now and for the rest of my life no matter how long or short it lasted.

I reached for the book in my pocket. It was her notebook filled with her poems. Worn and aged I placed it on the table next to her.

I was filled with a need to share something intimate with her. "You are a poet," I said to her proudly. "And your son is a poet, too. But you know that, don't you?"

I forced a smile but it faded quickly. I moved even closer to her.

Her eyes remained dull as she looked at me. I wanted to break through the disease. I needed to know.

"Why?" I asked like a child would ask about the mysteries of the universe, my voice trembling.

Helen's eyes were blank and her expression just as remote.

"Why did you give me away?" I asked again.

This time I thought I saw her *see* me. I leaned in closer. "Mom?"

Her eyes brightened as if they were distant stars in the murky heavens, faded but alive with flickers of light.

"Why did you give me away?" I asked again.

She continued to stare to some far off place.

"Please, tell me," I whispered.

And then she said, "I saw him *touch* you."

A long moment passed before I could respond. At first I imagined I heard her speak but then I wasn't sure. The flicker in her eyes was there. I was sure I saw it.

"You saw him touch me?" I asked waiting for an answer.

But there was none. Her eyes went dull again right before me and she was gone.

I wanted to shout but I knew she couldn't hear me. I wanted to shove her back into my reality but I knew that was hopeless. Yet I knew she saw me. I knew her eyes locked and she *knew* me.

Was this disease a ploy? I thought. Was it like everything else in my life— a lie?

All I knew was that for that one moment she released me and allowed me to go on. She told me what I had to hear and what I had to know.

Helen tried to save me from the monster who was my father. My birth mother gave me up in order for me to survive.

I sat back. There was no wind only the cool early spring air. I looked up at the sun and closed my eyes and for the first time in my life I knew what the truth had been and I embraced it.

Thank you for reading.
Please review this book. Reviews
help others find Absolutely Amazing eBooks and
inspire us to keep providing these marvelous tales.
If you would like to be put on our email list
to receive updates on new releases,
contests, and promotions, please go to
AbsolutelyAmazingEbooks.com and sign up.

# About the Author

Richard Vetere's first novel *The Third Miracle* published first by Carrol & Graf and then by Simon & Schuster was named one of the best debut novels of the year 1997 by Library Journal and garnered rave reviews. Mr. Vetere was hired by Francis Ford Coppola to co-write the screenplay adaptation.

His novel *The Writers Afterlife* was published in 2014 by Three Rooms Press to a rave review by Publishers Weekly. His novel *Baroque* about Caravaggio's roommate Mario Minniti was published in 2010 by Bordighera Press. His novel *Champagne and Cocaine* was published by Three Rooms Press in May 2016.

Mr. Vetere was nominated for Pushcart Prizes in fiction in 2013 and again in 2014.

Ovcr the years Mr. Vetere has written screenplays and adaptations for Paramount, Warner Bros, New Line and Zoetrope. In 2012 he was elected Council Member for the WGA East for a two year term.

Mr. Vetere wrote the most viewed teleplay ever shown on CBS TV, *The Marriage Fool,* an adaptation of his own stage play of the same title.

Made in the USA
Las Vegas, NV
06 August 2022

52823203R00089